THE EN

Lucas Clay

ROD SHAHAN

outskirts
press

Dedicated in memory to my Brother

Tom

When all roads you travel eventually lead home

Table of Contents

Introduction

I welcome you back to the continuing Adventures of Lucas Clay. Think back to all the times in your life when you stop whatever your doing just to take in one of most colorful and spell bounding sunrises or the same in a magnificent sunset. Your imagination will run with the moment as you see the dark silhouettes of the horses or cattle grazing along the hilltop. You will then begin to see an Indian Chief sitting straight and tall on his horse with his decorated spear at one side towering above. By now you can see yourself on the same hill riding atop your best and most loyal steed.

Within these stories you will find yourself doing exactly that. Riding along with Lucas Clay and sharing his adventures from the time the sunrises up from the plains till its sets into the majestic mountains. Grab hold of the reigns and let your imagination take you into the life and times of Lucas Clay, a man who lives life to its fullest with all the pride and courage of a true American cowboy.

CHAPTER 1

Thoughts From The Saddle

Don't let growing older get the best of you by it consuming your every thought. If you let it take hold you will find yourself saying such crazy things like, "no, that looks awfully heavy", or perhaps, "I use too, but not now days", maybe even, "I guess I just cant remember, comes with age you know". Well I'll tell ya, I know several people who always say, "I can't" for several things and will use age as an excuse as to why they can't. Now I am not going say that I am above all these folks cause I'm not. I guess what I am saying is that I remember all I can and as far as the rest goes, I know my limitations. If I were down at the saloon or Miss Vicky's café in town talking like this everyone would be thinking to themselves, "what the heck is wrong with Lucas". But I wouldn't blame them one little bit, what with having gray hair and beard along with the normal battle scars of being a cowboy, a carpenter or just pretty much a jack of all trades most of my life.

As I sit here on my horse overlooking the ranch I get to thinking about what it would be like if I had done some things differently knowing I had choices to make at the time. If I had turned left instead of right would I even be sitting here looking over my ranch, or if I had taken the low road instead of the higher one, would there perhaps be sons and daughters on their horses beside me as we all look down upon our ranch that we share together. I am almost positive that I'm not the only ole coot that has thoughts like this, no matter if your mending fences, branding cattle or just stirring a camp fire, your gonna start thinking. As common as these thoughts are, a man needs to stop and see exactly what he does have, and this is one of the spots here at the ranch where I can sit and do exactly that. Besides if this wasn't meant to be, then back years ago the good Lord would have prompted me to go left instead of right or take that lower road, but he didn't. So I cant see him faulting me for the decisions I make, only what I do with them.

JESSIES RIDE

THE GREENHORN STALLION

ROD SHAHAN

CHAPTER 2

Jessies Ride

The Greenhorn Stallion

SPRING DOESN'T START very early here at the base of the Greenhorn, but by golly when it does it's a sight to behold. Its like the lord will get his paint brushes out and create a new picture every day so you can watch the progress as it arrives. This time of year new life crops up all over the place, and not just the land but also the calves out in my pasture, the fawns following their mothers through the forest, and the new additions to the horses on the mountain. My heart swells when I think about the horses, these magnificent animals that seem to glide through the hillsides and meadows like royalty.

This time of year and the horses takes my memory back several years ago when a new school teacher came to town. She was so energetic and full of life ready to take on anything whether it was tied down or not. I don't believe there was any tardiness or skipping school the whole time she was here cause the kids just loved they way she taught them. I think that was because Miss Jessie also had one heck of an adventurous side to her. She felt that books alone wouldn't teach you all you needed to know, so she had a field trip for almost everything she taught. If she was teaching money they would go to the bank, or a ship captain they head out to Jenkins pond, she even took them to the hardware store, the hotel and the local saloon when she was on the subject of business. I think the town got a little concerned as the revolutionary war was coming up so they took the canon from the town square and put it in the mayors barn. So once they got to that subject she took all of them out to a small creek with not more than six inches of water and about four feet wide. She threw an old wooden crate in the water and told them about Washington crossing the Delaware River. I have no idea what the heck she would have come up with for Christopher Columbus, I reckon back over Jenkins pond again which made us all thankful we weren't any closer to an ocean.

Ya know, just an old cowboy out here on the ranch I have often thought what it would be like to have a family out here with me. A wife that cooks and cleans and helps with the chores, and then watching the children play around the barn, running through the pastures and teaching them the rules of life. But then on the other hand I think what if that wife doesn't cook what I like to eat and the kids would be wandering off getting into trouble to where all I got done was yelling to out them to get back to the house. I know all of that is a learning thing and I suppose I wouldn't mind at all teaching them. I guess my point is if I were to have a daughter, it sure would be nice to have one like Miss Jessie, that's all I am trying to say.

One day I was riding into town cause I needed a few supplies, not much just some coffee, beans and salt for curing. I got to the general store and happened to notice that Miss Jessie was also walking up to the store. I tipped my hat and wished her a good day then opened the store door for her. After we both walked inside she turned to me and asked if I would happen to know of any horses for sale in town or even around the valley area. Of course taken off guard like this I fumbled around and told her I couldn't think of any right away but I would sure keep her in mind when I did hear something. Just before I was leaving I turned to Miss Jessie and told her about the horses on the Greenhorn having their fowls this time of year. I told her that I will be having several friends of mine come up to the ranch for a roundup like I always do this time of year and invited her up to help. Oh my gosh, I have never seen anyone so exited about something in a long time. I told her that just before its time for roundup I would get word to her and maybe she would like to come along with us. She almost screamed the word "Yes" to where the other folks in the store stopped and looked in awe.

Several weeks had passed since I had been into town for those supplies, I was just way to busy with my own livestock and getting several fences mended, and not to mention the corrals, barn, cabin and on and on. Every spring there is always a whole bunch of fixin to do after a long hard winter. One day in particular I remember taking advantage of a warm day with no wind and decided it was a good time to put some slats back up on the barn roof that an ice storm had torn off. I had been up there for about an hour and figured it was about time to go down to get some water and some more boards and nails. When I turned around towards the ladder my eye caught something running across the top of my south pasture. It took a second or two to focus in then saw it was a horse but it wasn't one of mine or even one I have seen before. I sat there and watched and even from this distance I saw it was a stallion, running like the wind then stopping ever so often then take off again till finally he ran over the hilltop of the pasture and then he was out of sight.

More than likely it was one from the wild herd

further on up the mountain and got to wandering off on his own. I scrambled on down the ladder and went inside the barn to fetch more supplies to finish the job. Getting my supplies then walking on out of the barn while trying to balance all the boards in my arms, I heard a voice yell out "Afternoon Mr. Clay". Well I was so taken by surprise by the voice alone and certainly wasn't expecting anyone. I had stopped so quickly and looked around, I dropped everything in my arms then stumbled over the boards I just dropped. As I sat on the ground with a bunch of wooden slats around me I looked up and there was Miss Jessie on horseback and behind her were the Montgomery sisters Kacy and Kelly. They all three sat there in silence with a touch of red faces trying desperately to hold back their laughter.

Noticing their grins I stood up so fast they didn't have time to even start a chuckle. I looked at all of them with a serious look and said "afternoon ladies, and what do I owe the pleasure of this visit". I think they might have thought saying anything about the tumble might not be in order so Miss Jessie spoke up saying "Well Mr. Clay , Kacy and Kelly here was telling me that they had gone on a few roundups with you in the past and told me they would be happy to accompany me out here to your ranch to speak to you about the next one, because I remember you telling me about it back at the store a few weeks ago". I told her, " I would be happy to talk about the roundup so why don't the three of ya tie your horses over at the corral and we will have some cold water on the porch and talk it over". As they were taking their horses to the fence I gathered all the slats and piled them up against the barn wall then walked up to the cabin to fetch a pitcher of cold water and some cups.

While I was getting things ready for our talk on the porch I was wondering if maybe the Montgomery sisters were wanting to go on the roundup again or just showing Miss Jessie where I lived, I guess it didn't matter anyway. But she sure picked a couple of nice girls to be friends with cause they were always as polite and shy just like her, almost like the three of them could be sisters. While they were walking around pointing at different things just talking and a few giggles I brought some cold water out to the porch and some week old cookies for something extra. I said to the girls, "come on up here and grab a seat and we will see what we can come up with". They came gathering around and picking out the chairs they wanted to sit in and I just simply leaned up against the railing waiting to see who was going to start talking first.

Miss Jessie started out the talk by saying "It sure is a nice day isn't it Mr. Clay, in fact I'll bet you have a hard time leaving this place for even a day

because of all the fresh air and mountain views" .
Then Kelly Montgomery spoke up with a loud voice,
" Oh come on Jessie lets get down to business and
leave the small talk for later, Kacy and I need to
be back in town before nightfall". Well Kelly certainly has always been the outspoken one whether
you like her opinion or not, you are going to hear
it. Jessie quickly spoke up again and told me she
wanted to go on the roundup and even more so after
their ride up here. She told me that on the way here
they stopped and watched a white stallion running
towards the Greenhorn and asked me if I had seen
him or perhaps if he were one of mine. I told her
"well now Miss Jessie, I did see him and he is not
one of mine, I believe he is part of the wild herd that
goes to the higher meadows this time of year, "but
if your thinking what I think your thinking, then just
forget it".

   "Sorry Mr. Clay, I cant just forget it" she ex-
claimed, " and now that I know he is not one of
yours and is part of the wild herd that you have a
roundup on, then I am claiming him as mine to you
and my two friends here". I was taken off guard by
her sternness but you might figure that comes with
being a school teacher for several years. So I replied, " Ok Miss Jessie, if your going to claim him
then your going to help catch him, and that means
your gonna have to break him also". Then I asked "

Have you ever done anything like this before"? Boy howdy did she ever start belting out qualifications one after another, like when she helped her father on cattle drives and even competed in a few roping contest. But telling me wasn't enough, she walked off the porch and jumped on her horse then with a kick and a yell she took off at a full run straight towards my pasture gate with her rope twirling above. I would never have believed it if I hadn't have seen it with my own eyes, she roped the lever on the gate and opened it up all the way back.

Kacy looked at me and said "Well Lucas, I hate to say it but I think she will give even you a run for your money when it comes to roping". By golly I would never have guessed that a lady school teacher could ride and rope like that. So I had to admit to Kacy, "I believe your right, but don't you ever say I said that". So when Miss Jessie rode back to us I told her," your roping is some of the best I have seen, so our roundup is going to start in about five days, so be here next Monday morning if you want to see your dream come true, and make sure you are here at sunrise". I turned to the Montgomery sisters and asked them if they were going to be here also and they let me know very quickly that hell or high water couldn't keep them away from the first day of roundup.

The three of them rode off just as quick as they

arrived leaving me standing there thinking just what have I gotten myself into. For the first day of wild horse roundup I have two female wranglers and a lady school teacher as my starting line on the herd. Even though I have never come across this before, I have seen with my own eyes and past experience that these ladies have all the ability that any cow-poke would need in order to get the job done. So as the days drew closer to roundup I began getting ev-erything ready for the big day. All my tack and ropes worked down and thinking about the jobs each rider should have.

It seemed like no time at all the week had passed and the first day of roundup had finally got here. I had everything done around the ranch before sun up and was waiting on the porch with my coffee for my crew to arrive. Then finally I saw three riders coming down the road followed by a huge cloud of dust. I should have guessed it, my first arrivals were the Montgomery sisters and Miss Jessie.

These girls rode up front of the porch and the first thing out of their mouths was "when we heading out Lucas"? I told them we weren't going anywhere until Buck and Jim Bolz get here. Both the sisters looked at me at he same time and said, "Jim Bolz". I told them they heard me correctly and that its no se-cret that the two of them are sweet on him. But I also reminded them that today is roundup for horses and horses only. No sooner than I said that here comes my last two wranglers riding over the hill towards the cabin. I introduced Buck and Jim to Jessie and of course they already knew the Montgomery sisters. Everyone knew exactly what their job was except Miss Jessie, so I told her to stay close to me that I would guide her through it. I also told everyone that there is a white stallion up there and Miss Jessie has laid claim on him. This didn't seem to hurt anyone's feelings so we took off towards the Greenhorn with as much excitement as an ole cowpoke on payday heading to the local saloon.

Once we got to the ridge overlooking the high meadows we all sat there in a line looking at one of the most amazing sight. There must have been over a hundred horses grazing down there. Colors of all sorts and several yearlings, some moving ever slowly while most were content to graze in one spot. We were all ready to take our places and bring at least half of them down to our corrals. But Jessie spoke up and said, "wait, we cant go down yet, I don't see the white stallion anywhere". I told her to not worry cause no sooner than we get down there, he will be out in the open trying to protect his herd. So Buck and Jim took to left, the Montgomery sisters went right, then Jessie and I headed ever so slowly straight down towards the middle of the herd. Miss Jessie and I stopped short so that the others could herd them in the direction we wanted them to go. Then all the sudden Miss Jessie raised up in the stirrups and yelled out, "there he is, there's my white stallion".

I looked up towards the line of tall pines and sure enough here comes the white stallion at a full run like a momma bear protecting her cubs. He ran towards the front of the herd trying to direct them back to the forest where he knew there was safety. Like all heads of a herd he was doing his duty and so I knew if he were to be at the end of my lasso it was going to be a battle like no other. I had promised Miss Jessie my help, so I reckon a battle is on its way. I gathered my rope in hand and headed down the hill towards our white stallion, with Jessie running by my side with her lasso swirling above her.

The rest of our wranglers were working their positions by keeping most of the herd heading down the draw towards the ranch while Jessie and I were steadily making our way towards the infamous Greenhorn Stallion. I swear this horse was trying everything to out maneuver us at every turn. Suddenly Miss Jessie rode off towards the tree line disappearing into the pines stopping me dead in my tracks. Then like a hawk after its prey she comes charging out of the trees directly behind the stallion. As God is my witness I watched this young school teacher throw a ten foot circle over the neck of that wild stallion while bringing her horse to sliding stop. I rode over to her as fast as I could and threw my lasso over him. We were both keeping tension on our ropes trying to work him down. It seemed as if nothing else mattered at this time, we had almost forgot about the rest of the herd and my other wranglers. I was simply focused on bringing this stallion to the ranch for breaking and not concerned about the rest of the herd at all.

As time and patience did its job, the stallion was wearing down, almost to the point where he was keeping a slow but steady pace in front of us. We kept are ropes tight on him while slowly riding down the pasture towards the rest of our group.

We were both steadily guiding the stallion further down the pasture then Jessie yelled out to me, "Lucas, take your rope off of him, I will take him down myself". My first thought was, not a chance, but I knew how strong willed this girl was so I rode in and flipped my lasso from the stallions neck, leaving Miss Jessie as the only control over this strong animal . I was riding as close as I could in case my rope needed to come in handy once more. But to my surprise the stallion seemed to be subject to any direction Jessie were to take him. The further we rode down the hill I was in awe as to the ease which Miss Jessie was taking control and the submission which this great wild beast was letting itself be led by this gracious and meek school teacher.

Once I felt she had full reigns on the situation I rode on ahead and met up with the Montgomery sisters to make sure the rest of the herd was following their path. I rode over to Kelly who was stopped on a high spot and told her about Jessie bringing the stallion down by herself. She thought I was crazy as a sick coyote letting her do that by herself and started to head back up the hill to help her. I yelled out at her, "you stay right here Miss Kelly, you will see when she get down here, that girl has a natural way with these horses like I have never seen since you and Kacy started these roundups with me." So she stayed with me and told me , "I sure hope you are right Lucas".

No sooner than saying that here comes Miss Jessie with the white stallion in front of her still roped and leading the way she wanted. I looked over across the draw and saw Kacy atop her gray mare , which she was so proud of, watching as Miss Jessie was guiding that white stallion down the draw towards us with all the ease of a pro. She waved her hat in the air and yelled out "That a girl Jessie".

Evening was starting to creep up on us and we still had almost an hour before getting this herd into the pasture down at the ranch. I figured I better see if Jessie needed to be relieved from holding the stallion for a while cause that's an awful lot of strain on a small girls arm, plus loosening her saddle. When

I turned around I couldn't believe my eyes. Miss Jessie had dismounted her horse and was standing in front of the stallion rubbing his head and talking to him. I rode up on her extra slow so not to scare the horse and Miss Jessie. I then asked her in a very calm voice, "What in the heck do you think your doing girl, that is a wild horse". She simply looked over at me with a little grin and replied, " Wild, these horses are wild only if you tell them they are and treat them like they are." That comment made me dumb founded and speechless for about a minute till I realized I was looking straight at the proof of her logic.

I then asked " Miss Jessie just what are you going to do next". She looked up at me with a most serious look and said, "Mr. Clay, if you would be so kind as to take the lead rope of my horse, I believe I will ride this Greenhorn stallion down to your ranch, that's what I am going to do next". I tried every which way possible and all kinds of reasoning with her but it was like talking to an old oak tree. I started looking around for Kacy and Kelly but they were a bit further down the draw for them to hear me. As desperate as I felt to keep her from riding this stallion my heart felt that she could do it and do it very well. I reached over and grabbed the reigns of her horse then backed up a few feet so I wouldn't be in her way. I believe even my own horse was as unsure as I was with his twisting and turning. "OK" I said to Miss Jessie, "lets see how far you can go". She took a piece of rope, made a few knots then put it around the horses head for a halter and single reign. She looked over at me with a nose curling grin and said, "How about Mr. Clay, lets rodeo". She grabbed a hand full of mane with one hand while holding tight onto the rope with the other then swung herself up on that stallions back. That young horse did a whole lot of crow hoping and running in circles, but to my amazement he didn't buck once. This hopping around in circles didn't last anymore than a few minutes till Jessie had him going in the direction she wanted. It was as if she was riding one of our regular ranch horses bare back.

As I followed her down the draw I watched every move the stallion made and noticed every reaction Jessie made in response to the stallion. I knew without a shadow of a doubt I was witnessing a true natural spirit with a horse. She stopped that horse on a dime and turned towards me yelling out, "see you down at the ranch Mr Clay". She held on to the long flowing mane of that stallion and they took off down the hill like an eagle gliding steadily and free with the wind to their backs. I pushed my hat further down on my head, told ole Ruger, "lets go boy", and took off down the hill tying to keep Jessie and her stallion close by.

A few hundred yards down we were coming

upon the herd and I could see Kacy and Kelly off either side waving their hats in the air and yelling like a race was going on. Then within a split second the herd started following Jessie and the stallion down that hill keeping up the same pace and the same gracefulness as the gliding eagle. The Montgomery sisters followed behind them still waving their hats in the air and yelling out encouragement as if the finishing line was within sight. I could even see Buck and Jim who had stopped to see what all the excitement was about. I swear I could see the whites of there eyes all the way from back here because they were so wide open in amazement.

We were all trying to keep up with the herd and making sure none of them were leaving the trail. But for some reason I believe we all could have stopped where we were and simply watched this once in a life time event. As we were getting closer to the ranch I rode off to a small hill not far from the back of my corrals and sat in the saddle so I could watch the last few moments of this years roundup. And what a memorable roundup this is, one that will be talked about for years around campfires, dinner tables and even benches on the town square. I was seeing Miss Jessie on a proud white stallion riding like the wind towards the ranch with at least fifty more wild horses following behind her. I watched as some of the best horsemen around who were also some of my best friends riding along all sides of the herd twirling there hats in the air and yelling through those ear to ear smiles.

If anyone were to ask me how this years roundup went, the only answer I would have is, "you would had to have been there". And so you can only imagine what is going through this old cowboys mind and heart as I sit and take in this spectacular scene as I thank my God for giving me the memories of this day.

LAKOTA SUNRISE

A JOURNEY TO REDEMPTION

BY
ROD SHAHAN

CHAPTER **3**

Lakota Sunrise

A Journey to Redemption

IF YOU ARE early to a cattle auction it's a good thing, or if your early to an ice cream social it's a good thing, but if you get up to early here at the ranch and especially if you stayed up till midnight feeding an orphan calf, then that is not a good thing. But I will be dang if I am going to whine cause that little calf needed my help to survive and I need him as part of my herd. So the coffee is done, I'm all dressed' and in a little while some daylight is gonna be shining through the tall pines and that little calf will be out in the barn hollering for more food. So out on the porch I go with my hot coffee and a two day old biscuit waiting for the sun to give me a little more light. I sat my ole bones down in that squeaky rocking chair and after taking a few sips of my magnificent cowboy coffee and taking in some of that clean mountain air, of course mixed in with a little cattle manure, but that's what gives it substance and the feel of home. A lot of the other ranchers around will say to me " You smell that Lucas, that's the smell of money". Never being much of one on the benefits of money, which also means never having much money, I was always truthful in my response and simply told them, "smells like cow crap to me partner". Maybe that's one of the reasons I like raising my own cattle rather going down to the auction, just too much money in the air for such a small place. It was getting a bit lighter outside so I took my cup back inside and fixed a meal for that hungry calf, plus there are some hungry horses in the corral and cattle in the west pasture that need attention also. There has been a whole lot of these days that you just cant beat, the sun will rise, the calves will holler, the livestock need attention and then there is the horses. What can I say about my horses, other than this place may go to pot if they weren't around. Just try to imagine yourself walking fences with an arm full of tools and wire or putting a harness on your back and pulling a wagon into town, or perhaps try to roundup a herd of cattle while running in your boots and twirling a rope over your head. I don't think I would last very long, nor would anyone else.

Throughout my years here on the ranch working the land and livestock, I have never once took lightly my cowboy life, the beautiful mountains with the lush meadows, and the clean flowing water rushing down from the Greenhorn giving life to the entire valley. At the same time I am reminded that in some of the larger towns back east they have water running through a pipe and into their house, they will pull a little chain and a little glass bulb will light up the room. They have even brought their outhouses inside, that's the one I really need to question. Sometimes its sad to think they will never know the true circle of life, to see, hear and touch the natural things around them. Being the grandson of a Lakota woman, listening to her songs and stories, is why I have always felt like I knew the needs of my land and the animals that live here.

The calf has been fed, the horses are happy, I have Ruger saddled up and on my way to the pastures to check on the cattle. Today turned out to be a windy one but I wasn't hearing the loud squall of the windmill, so that's the first place I headed to in case its broke and no water in the tank. Just as soon as I topped the ridge the windmill was in sight and it was turning and pumping water like a new one. I try to grease it at least every week but it still gets loud no matter what. But this time its turning fast and not a sound out of it. I saw the tank was full so I tied up my horse and climbed up the windmill so I could tie down the blades in this high wind. I bet I struggled with that dad burn thing for the longest time, trying to hold it steady and hook the stop lever, but just as soon as I almost have it hooked a strong gust of wind would flip it around again. A slight calmness seemed to come about so I moved to the other side of the platform to grab the darn thing and bring it back to me. Just as soon as I had a firm grip on it a huge gust brought it flying straight at me. Holding my arm out and trying to hold onto the rig didn't help a bit. That blade tail hit me so hard all I could see was the sky and me flying through the air.

When something like this happens you have absolutely no control of the outcome, it's either a hard landing or a soft landing, and a soft landing is very doubtful. Lets just hope I survive it, just like when we would bust the bronc's, or ride a few bulls for the heck of it. I don't think I saw my entire life flash before my eyes, or even the face of an angel calling me. But I very well could have, cause a thousand thoughts went through my head within five second before I hit the ground. Why, I even saw Ruger standing there calmly watching me go down.

Then I felt the hardest thud to these ole bones and all my air was knocked out of me in an instant. I laid there gasping for even the slightest amount of air and watching the clouds blowing past overhead. I certainly didn't know whether I was awake, knocked out or in heaven. I don't really know just how long I laid there in utter silence and not feeling a thing in or around me. But what seemed to be forever I then heard a voice in the distance, then the voice got louder and louder till I could make out someone calling my name, "Lucas, Lucas". Then with my eyes barely open I saw a blurry figure knelt over me and their firm grip on my shoulders shaking me and calling my name. By golly I knew I wasn't a goner cause I don't think God would be shaking my shoulders while asking me "you ok Lucas, you ok". He would have just shook my hand, gave me wings and said "Welcome Home Cowboy".

That may have been a good thing, but in this case it wasn't time for that. So for now I was being shaken and yelled at and not to mention a few slaps on either side of my face. I was wishing I would come to a little faster so as not to put up with this abuse. Then slowly but surely my vision started to become more clear where I could make out the person calling my name. I was expecting one of my neighbors or my friend Buck who helps me at the ranch most of the time, but it wasn't either one of them.

With so much light in my eyes all I could see was his silhouette, which gave way to a lot of long hair blowing in this strong wind. My senses slowly started to come back to me till finally I began to recognize the voice. This man grabbed hold and pulled me up onto my feet asking the whole time if I could stand and if I were alright. I made it to my feet but shaky as a new born calf, then I asked "is that you Tall Bull"? Then with the authority of a school teacher he said to me "Lucas you set down on this rock and let me take a look at you". Right now I didn't know what the heck to think, other than I wanted to fix the windmill then got hit by the blade and fell to the ground getting knocked out cold.

While sitting on the rock with my head hanging down and still in a state of confusion I received a quick, cold shock of water being poured over the back of my neck. I tell you what that state of confusion sure made way to reality in a second. I stood and said, " that is you isn't it Tall Bull", you're the only ole cuss I know that believes cold water thrown on you is the cure for everything. Being a stubborn man of a few words his reply was obvious, "It worked didn't it, your standing and you will dry off quick in this wind".

Tall Bull walked over to my horse and grabbed the rope from my saddle, talking a whole bunch of Sioux at the same time, he threw one end over the blade on the windmill and securely tide it to the braces below. After mumbling a bunch more he walked over to me and said, "now lets get you on your horse and we will go back to the cabin and make sure your ok". While he was helping me back to Ruger I tried telling him that I still needed to make sure the cattle was doing ok in the upper pasture. Very firmly he told me " Lucas, I saw them on my way down here and they are fine, now lets go to the cabin".

With all that being said I saw no reason to start going against Tall Bulls wishes, after all I really didn't feel as if I could make it to the pasture anyway. We both started down the hill headed towards the cabin with Tall Bull right beside me in case I had a whim to fall off my horse. While we were riding down the hill my thoughts were taking me back when I first met Tall Bull. My grandmother had told me about my Lakota relatives living in the Dakota territories. Several years ago I was part of a surveying expedition marking out the perimeter of the Standing Rock Sioux reservation. One day we were surveying the north boundary and I needed to ride to the highest point north where I could see the crew along with the western plateaus.

I remember sitting on my horse and looking off into the vast valley below when I saw another rider just sitting on his horse atop the ridge just east of me. My thinking was that he had been sitting there for awhile watching me the whole time. Of course I couldn't quite make out who the man was, I just figured he was probably part of my crew. It didn't bother me much so I proceeded to place a marker at this point because from here I could see the furthest perimeter. Once I climbed back on my horse and looked again to find the rider, I could not see him anywhere, so I started riding back down the hill in order to catch up to my crew.

I didn't get any further than a few hundreds yards down the hill and around some huge rocks when I came upon a man sitting tall on his horse right in the middle of my path. I could see that he was Sioux so my defense instincts started to kick in. I quickly pulled my Winchester out and demanded he stop and tell me what he is doing here, while at the same time looking around to see if any of his friends were sneaking up around me. I called out to him " I am a US government surveyor, what do you want". And so to my surprise he responded back with " I know what a surveyor is white man, do I look stupid to you, I have been watching you most of the day". That man was Tall Bull and we have been friends ever since.

Crazy how you think about things when your hurting so dang much that you normally wouldn't otherwise. But I still kept looking over towards Tall Bull to make sure it really was him, after what I just been through I could have been seeing rabbits riding billy goats, you just never can be to sure. We finally got to the cabin and Tall Bull gave me a helping hand down off the saddle and we tied our horses to the post for the time being. He thought I might need a hand getting up the steps to the porch, but I quickly told him "No dad burn it, I don't need a hand getting into my own house". So he backed off a little and when I got to the top step I headed straight to my rocking chair and sat down. I told Tall Bull he might as well sit in the other one cause I was not getting up for a little while till I have a little more senses about me. We sat there for the longest time in silence looking off into the distance, but every now and then I could tell he was still keeping a close watch on my behavior just in case the head knockin was more than he thought. I was really starting to feel just fine so I looked over at him with my stiff neck cocked over to one side and said " Will you please quit doing that". "Doing what" he replied. I told him "You keep looking over at me like your expecting me to fall out of my chair, but I am feeling just fine, ok". Well in his usual self he pulled a rag from his pocket and threw it onto my lap then told me "Here, because your just fine you wipe the blood off your forehead yourself". I ran the rag over my brow and sure enough I was bleeding . It didn't seem to be that big of a cut and besides I think he said that just to rib me a bit. So I finished wiping off my brow with his rag then tossed it back at him after I was done followed by a simple thank you. But now comes the time that I need to know why Tall Bull is here. I sat up a bit taller in my chair and turned towards him and said " Tall Bull, you are my blood brother and close friend, and I haven't seen you since the pow-wow at the reservation five years ago, and now today if you hadn't have shown up I would still be laying in tall grass knocked out and bleeding."

After all these years it was good to see Tall Bull no matter what the reason but still I simply asked, "Tall Bull, tell me what brings you here". For the longest time he just sat there looking far away as if his answer was going to arrive any minute, perhaps coming down the road or even dropping out of the sky. So just as soon as I opened my mouth to say something he belted out "Its Little Owl Lucas, He is gone". Of course thinking that something had happened to him like he had died from sickness or even been killed by enemy or an accident, I responded " Tall Bull, I am so sorry, Little Owl was my brother also, What happened that took him from us"? Within his slow deep voice I could see he was struggling with the explanation, then with only a few seconds he finally said, "He is not dead Lucas, He has only been taken and I must get him back.

"Tall Bull you need to tell me what happened" I replied. He stood up and walked over to the rail of the porch as if he needed something to hold onto while he gave me the story behind Little Owl being gone. He proceeded to tell me that he and Little

Owl were gone for several days checking on the traps they had laid and looking for any signs of buffalo near the Black Hills close to their home. "Only a few buffalo were to be seen Lucas and our traps were gone, as if someone had stolen them". As he told me this I remember hearing that hundreds of white men have been shooting buffalo for their hides and horns only, and then bragging about their fearless hunts. But I know that this had nothing to do with Little Owl being gone.

He turned towards me pointing towards his chest and hitting it several times saying "You remember this Lucas, remember what the Cheyenne did to me"? And like a rock hitting me in the head the memory of Tall Bull being captured and tortured by some renegade Cheyenne several years ago came to me as clear as if it were yesterday. I told him, "yes I do remember, and I also know that you must still bear the scars on your chest and your soul".

Many thoughts came to me at this time but only one big one, and that was the Cheyenne have taken Little Owl and I am going to grab some rations and as much ammunition as possible. So when I stood up waving my arms and yelling in vengeance Tall Bull knew that I was ready to go to war cause it looked like the pains from the fall have all gone away. He took hold of me and said "Lucas, let me finish, and then you decide if its war or not". As I told you before when we arrived at our traps they were all gone and no signs of the beaver or musk rat taking them away. After all I can see one beaver taking a loose trap down stream or even a musk rat caught in one and a bear or coyote taking him and the trap. But I can not see all of them being taken this way. And if it were a white trapper they would leave signs that even a baby could see.

I stood there listening and trying to imagine every step they took but so far I wasn't hearing anything about Little Owl. I stepped in with, "Where is Little Owl" and where are the Cheyenne?" Tall Bull told me to let him finish. He continued by saying Little Owl was with him and just as puzzled about the traps. So they rode a little ways down stream and saw no signs then came back and did the same going upstream. He said no matter where they looked there were not signs of missing traps or even why they were missing. Then with a moment of silence and his fist shaking he said, "Then I saw my sign". Thinking to myself that if any being on earth were to find an invisible sign it is the Lakota Sioux, and Tall Bull is one of the best there is. He is the man who taught me how to track a rabbit in a blizzard or even know everything about a horse and his rider just by looking at the hoof print. "What did you see"? I asked. He told me with the sunlight shining across the stream he saw a faint glitter shaking in the breeze on one of the cottonwood trees so he immediately rode over to look. Riding to the spot where he saw the glitter he saw a reddish colored object shining on a branch. He pulled it away from the branch and looked at a single small bead which he knew right away was from a Cheyenne blanket garnish.

I was trying my best to take in and understand everything that Tall Bull was telling me but I sure need for him to get straight to the point. I started to back away from the idea of war and was thinking more of finding Little Owl no matter what its gonna take. I believe I heard enough about what had happened and now I just wanted to take care of what I can do. So straight forward I asked Tall Bull, "What is it you wish for me to do, because I will ride hard and directly into the face of an enemy in order to save my young brother". Tall Bull replied " Lucas we must go forward with the Great Spirit as our guide then our body and soul will take and conquer what ever lies ahead". For some reason I knew because of this deep feeling within my gut that this was going to be a life changing or even a life ending adventure.

I believe the both of us realized what needs to happened and the action we need to take, and that is we need to make plans to get our brother back. I told Tall Bull that it's to late in the day to start out on the trail, so we need to get a fresh start tomorrow.

With what daylight we had left I needed to ride over to my neighbor Bucks ranch and tell him I would be gone for a while and ask if he would take care of the place while I was gone. So I told Tall Bull, " come on, lets to Bucks place and see if he will look after the place for a while".

Almost as if he had heard us through the trees here comes a rider down the road heading to the cabin, and I will be dog if it wasn't ole Buck. Coming in quick with the dust stirring, Buck yelled out "Is everything alright around here"? "Yep, everything is alright here Buck", I replied, "in fact we were just getting ready to come and see you". I told him that my brother Tall Bull and I had some business to take care of up north in the Dakotas and it would sure be nice if he would watch out over the ranch while I was gone. Of course Buck had no problem with that but sure had a puzzled look on his face.

There aren't too many things that will slide past Buck no matter what the subject, and then its that intuition he has about something that is going to happen or knowing what has happened without being told. And right now is a prime example of this because he comes riding up almost like he knew something was wrong and I haven't even seen him in several days. God sure did bless this man with a gift and I am glad he's my neighbor and friend. I knew Buck wouldn't settle for just the business excuse, so I told him to come up on the porch and let Tall Bull and I explain why I needed to be gone.

After telling him everything which Tall Bull had told me, Buck's only words were "I see". I looked at him in amazement then responded, "Is that all you can say, is, I see", I know you better than that". Buck continued on by saying " Lucas, about five years ago you remember you and I went to Wyoming and brought back some mustangs from the Big Horn area. "Yes, I told him and that is when you first met Tall Bull and Little Owl, wasn't it". He told me, " it certainly was and if it wasn't for those two we would be buzzard bait because the Cheyenne thought we were stealing those horses, then Tall Bull here and his brother told them they were Sioux horses, and we know the Cheyenne didn't want to fight the whole Sioux tribe". Well it sounded like Buck remembered every detail of that trip and wasn't about to forget what Tall Bull and Little Owl did for us.

So now with everything being told I asked Buck if he would still look out after the ranch while I was gone. He looked at me and asked "remember my son Dean"? "Yes I do", I replied. He continued saying, "Well he is staying at the ranch and knows everything about the chores, supplies and what needs to be done, and not only my ranch but yours as well". I believe I knew what he was getting at, so I said to him, "Well by golly Buck in that case if you would like to ride with me and Tall Bull in search of Little Owl it would sure be appreciated".

With a grin on his face it didn't take but a second for him for to say, "You darn right I will go", I knew Buck would be a good hand to come along so I told him to be back here by first daybreak tomorrow morning. Buck climbed back on his horse and said "Lucas , Tall Bull, I'll see you boys in the morning", then he rode away as fast as he came in. I turned to Tall Bull and told him we need to get rations and make a few plans for the days ahead of us. I knew we couldn't take a pack horse because of riding quick and silent so stuffing as much into our saddlebags as possible but making room for ammo, which seemed to be the main cargo. This isn't the first time I have taken off with a lot more bullets than food. Besides when your out on the trail food in most cases is everywhere around you, but ammo isn't.

Tall Bull and I spent the evening making plans and even backup plans for any situation that came up and our supplies were laying beside the door ready to pick up and go. With a restless sleep that seemed to have lasted forever I finally had to get up make ready for the day. I wasn't a bit surprised that Tall Bull was already outside getting his horse ready. I told him that some old biscuits were laying on the stove and yesterdays coffee was there also. And just before we started back inside here comes the sound of a horse running down the road, and with a whirlwind of dust flying around him we heard Buck yell out "you fellas ready to go"?

I told Buck to climb on down and grab some coffee while I put some more things in my bags. Just as we were ready to go I told Buck " you being with us will help the chances of finding Little Owl a lot more, but I also want you to know that there is also a chance that we may not come back home alive". Buck told me that this wasn't the first time we have taken out somewhere knowing the same thing. So with the sun barely rising and the moon hanging over the west, the three of us took off on our mission, a mission that could very well change our future and others as well.

We were approaching the Wild Horse plateau when the sun finally shined brightly over the eastern foothills and our trail laid just over the next ridge. I turned my horse around and stood there for a little while looking back towards the Greenhorn mountain where the ranch spread out along its base and the pastures where the wild horses gathered. I guess I was wondering if I would ever see this again or not. Several memories rushed past me like thumbing quickly through a book, except this book was my life on this vast area before me. Then suddenly these thoughts went away just as quickly as they came to me, because the face of Little Owl appeared to me when he was a young boy and then when he became a brave. Without a doubt I knew that his safety for the sake of the tribe was more important to me than my own.

I turned my horse back around and there was Tall Bull looking at me almost like he knew what I was thinking. He said " Lucas, the Great Spirit was talking to you wasn't he". I replied by telling him "Tall Bull, no matter what this journey brings, just know that Little Owl will be going home, and , YES, he did tell me our journey was good". With Buck looking towards us he yelled out "Are you guys coming or not"? So with my objective set in stone I told Buck "Yep, we're coming, lets head to the trail, we have a job to do".

The three of us rode off towards the opening in the trees which led to the northern prairie. Once we cleared what was left of the small patches of Ponderosa pines and rode to the next ridge we saw our journey before us, from one horizon to the other as far as we could see the tall grass was blowing in the breeze like the ocean waves and a single tree placed ever so often in the distance. "This is the beginning of our journey to find Little Owl" said Tall Bull. With the three of us looking onward we began our ride northward with confidence knowing we had the help of the Great Spirit.

Its been darn warm for this early in the spring, even the snow caps didn't cover as much this year. The creeks were barely flowing back home but at least they had some water in them. I was a little worried that we wouldn't have any water or green grass but looking out across the plains there was a green tint to the grass which meant there is some decent grazing for our horses. There ain't many creeks or watering holes in the prairie but as long as the ones we know about aren't dried up and the old stage stop near Broken Wheel hasn't been burnt down, we should be just fine.

Now the stage stop at Broken Wheel should be running fine and dandy cause I have known the proprietor for several years and this lady is as tuff as a cornered bob cat, you open that door the wrong way and you had better stand back or Miss Lora is gonna tear you to shreds. She came to this territory several years ago with her husband Elroy from back east somewhere around Boston. I don't think they were town folk cause she knows to much about country life and surviving. And that was obvious when her husband told her one morning he was riding into Baxter Bend to get a few supplies and never came back. That's been several years ago and I have never known what happened and she has never talked about it. Every now and then I have heard some stories back home about her sending some outlaws to their maker and some Cheyenne renegades wishing they had never come across the stage stop.

We were starting to top a high point on the trail then Tall Bull stopped and turned around towards Buck and I. He pointed towards a low area with a few trees and told us he will ride down to scout because this was our first chance at water and breaking camp for the night. "You and Buck wait here as lookouts and I will be back" he told us. So Buck and I dismounted and let our horses rest while we kept a watch on Tall Bull and the surrounding area. From where we stopped you could see several miles in any direction, so if were anything taller than a jack rabbit out there, we would see it.

We probably waited for at least a half hour till we saw Tall Bull riding hard our direction but off to the north a little. I couldn't figure out why cause he knew where we were. We soon saw why, there were two riders coming up over the hill not far behind him at such a full run they were starting to gain on him. "Cheyenne" I yelled out to Buck, "Lets get in behind them or Tall Bull wont make it". We made a running mount and headed towards them as fast as our horses could go. I went to the left and Buck went to the right and as soon as we were within range and our Winchesters up and ready we both started firing at the same time. Those two braves were running so hard trying to catch Tall Bull I don't believe they knew we were there at all. But with the sound of a rifles they slowed to look around and that's all it took. Our pace was steady and our aim was right on, and those two braves fell to the ground.

We stopped where they were laying to make sure they weren't moving. They were for sure Cheyenne braves but they also had war paint on their faces and so did their horses. Tall Bull rode up to us looking at the two braves and told us what had happened. He said when he was approaching the group of trees at the water hole he saw signs that meant someone was there. So on foot he started walking a little closer when an arrow flew past barely missing him. He said he ran back to his horse and took off but not straight as us, knowing we would see all of them and come in behind the two braves.

I asked Tall Bull "Why the war dressing? He told me "you see the two black marks on their arms where one is straight and the other looks broken in the center, that means these two braves have been separated from the rest of the tribe like several others have done because they refuse to follow the decision of the elders". I asked him why he thought they were no longer with the tribe and he told me that the Cheyenne elders were wanting to make peace with the other nations and the white man, but these braves and others wanted no part of that, only vengeance.

Buck rode off after the two Cheyenne ponies so they wouldn't head back to the main camp, then we could take the braves up to some higher ground for burial because there was no way any of us could leave them lying there for the coyotes. The Cheyenne are just as proud and courageous tribe as the Lakota and so their death should be treated with the same respect. So when Buck came back with the ponies we placed them over there mounts and rode up to a spot where their remains should be placed. Then if the rest of their band were to find out what happened then they would know that we treated them with respect and honored their death.

We then rode back to the watering hole among the trees watching ever so closely to make sure there were no more surprises anywhere around us. While Buck and I were letting our horses water, Tall Bull thought he should finish his scouting by riding the outer line of the trees to see if there were any more tracks besides the two braves. It didn't take him long to come back to tell us that the tracks of the two braves was all he found and that they were probably scouting for the rest of the band. Sometimes the scouts will search a day or more from the rest of their band, almost like hawks searching for prey not concerning themselves with time.

We felt it was safe to set up camp here for the night and even have a fire for some food and warmth.

We made sure our horses had plenty of water then started in gathering some fire wood and getting a few rations from the saddle bags. We were all silent for the longest time as we sat looking into the burning embers. I broke the silence by saying "You know their friends will come looking for them but this time there will be a lot more then just two scouts". Then Buck spoke up and said "And that's why we need to leave here before sunup, we will have a full moon to ride by so I am thinking we could get several miles away before the sun comes up". Tall Bull and I agreed with him and also suggested we took turns taking watch throughout the night.

It was a very restless night when you try to get a little sleep then someone is shaking your shoulder telling you its your turn to take watch, but I reckon it wouldn't bother me if I stood watch all night. I was the last one to take watch before sunlight and it was also the most quiet time through out the night except for birds and a few coytes. I would look towards the campfire every now and then to make sure Buck and Tall Bull were still covered in their blankets. I then went over to our horses checking the ropes and calming them a little, thinking I should give them a hand full of feed before we hit the trail again. As I was going over to fetch some oats I had this feeling that something wasn't right with horses, then it hit me, there were only two horses on the rope.

I immediately turned around and started back over to them hoping that one of them was just a little further down in the dark. Getting closer I knew my eyes were not playing tricks on me and that Tall Bulls horse wasn't there. I searched around the tree grove looking in all directions but nothing. I ran back to the camp to wake my friends, but only Buck was laying beside the fire. I reached down and shook Buck yelling, " Buck wake up, Tall Bull is gone and so is his horse". It took Buck a few moments to come to his senses then he jumped up telling me "I knew this would happen, I just knew it". "What the heck you talkin about" I replied.

Buck told me that before we all settled in for the night he saw Tall Bull pulling a red feather from his pouch then walked over to his horse and spoke something while waving the feather over his horses head. He then came back over to the camp fire and sat down then started waving his feather again and chanting something but he couldn't make out what he was saying and just figured it was one of his rituals. "Lucas" he said "What the heck ya think is going on"?

When Buck told me about the red feather I knew that we were now on our own without Tall Bull so I explained to him the best I could. Knowing the Lakota ways and some of their beliefs I remembered the story of the Red Feather. When searching for a trail and asking the Great Spirit to show you the way, he will send you a red feather which will show you the direction to take. This feather symbolizes the lone Red Tailed Hawk which never looses sight of his journey and can see whatever lies ahead, . "For some reason" I explained to Buck, "Tall Bull must have had a vision about what lies ahead and knew he had to go alone, but right now I am not going to try and figure out what he saw or which direction he took cause we can find that out soon enough. But for now we know he is gone and we need to continue to search".

With only about an hour before sunrise we gathered our gear, put out the campfire and saddled our horses. At this point our plans were to head north where the Platte river joins the Salt Basin which is where Tall Bull said him and Little Owl were checking on their fur traps. From where we are now there is no way we can get there in less than a three day ride. So now I wonder, why did Tall Bull ride five days to the south just to get my help when he could have gone only one day east and half the tribe would be heading out to find Little Owl. I guess the answer to that will have to wait till we catch up to Tall Bull and ask him.

We took off heading due north with as much energy as a coyote after a rabbit. The sun was starting to make way over the eastern horizon and Buck and I were riding so steadily northward that we hardly noticed the storm clouds gathering overhead. But when we saw lightning strikes in the distance and felt a few rain drops on our faces, we stopped to look around and try to see which direction the storm was going. I doesn't take much to figure out that in a lightning storm on the prairie your probably the tallest thing out there.

We took off heading north towards Broken Wheel at a full run hoping to stay ahead of this storm but it seemed to be hopeless cause the faster we rode the closer the storm got. When your out here in the northern plains, trying to find shelter is like finding gold in your garden, It almost never happens. But to our surprise just a few miles ahead was a hill with what looked like a few trees and maybe even some rocks around it. So that's the direction we headed and hoping we don't get blown away before getting there.

We were riding hard towards that hill hoping it would be our shelter from this storm that was gaining on us closer and closer. I could see a wall of dust behind us hundreds of feet high with bolts of lightning streaming across the sky above it. I would rather have a stampede of a hundred buffalo behind me than this monster that reached up into the clouds. I could see two large boulders ahead of us with a single large cedar tree between them, and by glancing over to Buck, I knew he saw them also. So with our nose to the mane we were there within a few minutes and tied our horses to the cedar tree.

With only a moment to spare we took some gear off our mounts and tied some cloth around the horses eyes to protects them from the dust and to keep them a little calmer. We then wedged our selves down between the rocks and were still able to hold the ropes to the horses if they got too spooked. Then all of the sudden we were surrounded with dust and the loud roar of wind swirling around us. Trying to hold on to our horses and seeing through the blowing dust was one heck of an ordeal but I knew we could do it. Just as long as we had hold of our horses, even if they drug us out of the rocks, I knew we could make it through this. Then just as fast as it came upon us, the roar of the winds and the blinding dust left us traveling northward like a train in the night. The horses had calmed down some but we weren't about to leave our shelter, not for a while yet.

With a wall of rain water following the high winds we knew we weren't out of harms way cause it could have hail coming along with it. As we sat there listening to the storm it seemed like the noise was starting to quiet down a little. Buck decided to make his way out of the rocks and take a look around. He yelled back at me "Lucas, I can see blue sky to the south, I think this is all there is". I climbed out from the rocks after him looking back towards the south, sure enough some blue sky was behind the storm. Then all of a sudden the roar of a thousand lions deafened our ears and with the strength of a train we saw the beast of the prairie swirling around to our east, pulling up grass, dirt and anything else that was in its way. Lord oh mighty, this twister had touched ground only a few hundreds yards to the east of us and luckily its path was staying eastbound. But no matter how many blindfolds you tie on a horse they could hear that roar and the suction in the air that would take your breath away. Back home we would have some darn heavy snow storms in the winter and some heavy rain and hail come spring, but I sure cant remember any twisters until I left the mountains and rode off to the prairie.

We watched the twister as it headed further away leaving what looked like a wide wagon path behind. The rain was starting to slow down along with the winds so now is as good a time as any to hit the trail north again. As we rode around the base of this hill which served as our refuge in the storm, what we thought were more small trees, were not that at all, not one dog gone bit. This is sacred ground, they are actually burial platforms and no doubt Kiowa. We didn't dare go any closer, we sat there looking around in all directions for the longest time to make sure we weren't being watched. You would think in a storm like this there wouldn't be anyone around but when it comes to sacred ground, you never know. As long as we don't go past their warning sign which is usually a pole or spear with their tribal symbols, we should be ok and even keep what little hair we have.

We were riding at a slow and steady pace northward, constantly looking around to make sure we were still alone. As the sacred ground became ever so smaller in the distance then finally just a small spot on the horizon, we became more relaxed and started concentrating on the journey ahead. I believe the chances of us being spotted near that burial ground by anyone during a strong storm was pretty darn slim. We picked up the pace a little faster hoping to gain more ground which we lost during the storm and not even looking behind us. Even right now if any Kiowa were to find out we were there they would have to ride till their horses dropped cause we were so far ahead.

With perhaps a few hours left before sundown I knew it wasn't long before we rode into Wagon Wheel where Miss Lora ran the stage stop and it sure as heck wont be none to soon because the horses and us need some food, water and a good long rest. I told Buck that when we get to the stage stop that it is highly likely that we could get some news on Tall Bull or even a Cheyenne party may have been seen in the area, " It sure would help out a bunch", Buck replied," especially if we could catch up to Tall Bull again and find out just why in the heck he took off for anyway" . I couldn't have agreed more.

If my memory serves me correctly, just over this next hill we should be able to see Wagon Wheel along with anything or anybody around it. With some of the unrest in these parts you never want to just ride into a place without looking it over first. As we sat on high ground overlooking Wagon Wheel we saw no movement of any kind, no lights not even smoke from the chimney. I told Buck we should separate as we go down, "You ride down from the east and I will go down from the west, then lets meet at the barn across from the stage stop". So we each took off down the hill with me going my way and Buck going his. I sure hoped everything was ok down there and no danger came Miss Lora's way cause she sure was liked in these parts.

The closer I came to the old stage cabin I wasn't seeing any signs of life at all, not even livestock in the corrals. If the stage stop were working as usual there would surely be a few spare horses in the corrals. So before I went closer to the barn to meet Buck I decided to go a little further past our meeting place in order to see the back of the cabin. When I got closer to the back of the stage stop I saw one horse tied to a tree out back, this seemed to be awfully odd, so I immediately turned around to meet Buck over at the barn. So far it wasn't looking good here because no signs of people around and no horses in the corrals and one saddled horse behind the old cabin. It sure looks like someone is in that place and don't believe it would be Miss Lora, cause I would think she would put her horse in the barn.

I got back down to the barn and rode around back to meet Buck. He was already waiting there for me still mounted and holding his hand out in front of his face like he was telling me to be quiet. I rode up beside him and asked "What's wrong, what did you see"? He said that when he rode closer to the old mercantile store, which was the only other building here at Wagon Wheel, he could have sworn he saw someone walking from there to the stage stop cabin. Then I said, "You are probably right, cause I went around back of it and saw a saddled horse tied to a tree near the back door but I didn't see anyone around, not even any sounds of someone".

Because of everything we have seen, we decided to tie our horses here at the barn and walk over to the stage stop. Buck would go around towards the back and I would approach from the front. As soon as I knew Buck was in place at the back of the cabin I walked closer to the front porch and yelled out, "Is anybody there, hello in the cabin". I yelled out a second time and no sooner than I did a shot rang out in back of the cabin and then another one right after that. I started yelling out Bucks name and running to the back of the cabin as fast as I could.

While running towards the back all I could think of was that Buck got shot by who ever was inside, so with my Colt in hand I was ready to have the shooter meet his maker. When I cleared the corner of the cabin I was so relieved to see Buck standing there with his rifle pointing at someone on the ground. "Did you shoot em Buck" I yelled out. "Naw, he replied, " I saw him coming out the back door and only shot into the air, and this fellow hit the ground so dang hard he must have thought I shot him". I walked over to this guy and gave him a nudge with my foot telling him " now you get the heck up and show us who you are then tell us what your doing here.

He got up on his knees with his hands in the air, then while making it to his feet he said, "Don't shoot, please don't shoot". Buck and I looked at each other with a puzzled look on our faces and we heard the same thing, this is a woman's voice, and with it getting later in the day the shadows here behind the cabin made it hard to recognize a face. So my first response was "Who are you"? When she replied we knew that this was for sure a woman and Buck and I lowered our guns a little, but not to much cause a female out here in the west can be just as mean as anybody else.

When she stood up I saw there was a six shooter strapped around her waist so I quickly removed it from the holster and told her " I'll hold on to this for now, but you better start talking cause this place belonged to a friend of mine and from what I can see, you aren't her. She lowered her arms and said " you must be talking about Lora". "Yes I am" I replied, "now where is she"? She started telling us her name was Daisy and that Lora was her cousin. She continued saying " We were very close growing up and had always talked about having our own little store together but as we got older she came out west and I stayed home hoping one day I could do the same. So I sent her a letter saying I would be coming to Broken Wheel and maybe help her with the stage stop. But when I arrived a week ago no one was here.

At this point we started to let our guard down a little so I told Daisy that we need to go inside cause it sounds like there is a lot we need to talk about. Buck told me that he is going to tend to the horses and he would be inside directly. So I followed Daisy inside the cabin where she started to put some fire wood inside the cook stove while I began a fire in the fireplace. I had all sorts of things swarming around in my head so I turned to Daisy and asked, "

Why on earth have you been here for an entire week alone and not wanted to travel on"? She told me after arriving at Ft. Morgan on the train she was told the stage didn't go to Broken Wheel any longer and the only reason they gave was because they found a faster and safer route. Daisy told me she started asking around if anyone knew the way to Broken Wheel and all she got was shrugs or a few evil eyes. So she bought a horse from the livery stable and headed out on her own.

She said "I got no further than the outside of town and an Indian scout on his horse was in the middle of the rode and I was too scared to go any other direction cause I knew he would probably catch up to me, then he raised his hand and asked me If I was Daisy". "Holy cow" she said "this man knew my name and spoke very good English". She went on to tell me that he had heard her name in town and what she was looking for and that he knew the way to Broken Wheel. She said she felt like she could trust him so that is how she got here safely. I asked her to tell me more about the scout and she said "Lucas, that's the strange part, shortly after we got here he took a red tinted feather from his pouch and waved it around then stuck it in that tree out front. He turned towards me and told me I would be safe here and that Red Hawk would be coming soon. So Lucas I have been to afraid to go anywhere and afraid that his friend Red Hawk will be sneaking up on me from out of nowhere. And now you and your friend show up from no where, I guess I just don't know what to think or do".

I asked Daisy if she remembered anything about this scout, maybe his horse or even what he was wearing. She said he rode a paint horse but nothing unusual and that the scout wore buckskin. Although, she told me that he did have a long knife with a handle that looked like part of a deer antler. "Lucas" she said " this is the other strange thing, after he told me about this man Red Hawk, I went over to my bags to give him something for helping me out, but when I turned around he was gone, I looked in all directions and even ran over to the tree where he sat on his horse, and he was no where to be seen, I didn't even hear him ride off".

Many years ago after meeting Tall Bull, he started riding with me on some of the surveying jobs. Because I always knew my directions and about how far away something is, he would ever so often call me Red Hawk because of that. It was then that he told me that the feather of the Red Hawk will always point the way. I put these two things together, the antler handled knife and Red Hawk, and I knew without a doubt that the scout that led her here to Broken Wheel was Tall Bull. Just then Buck comes storming through the door and said "Lucas, you need to come outside, you need to see what I just found". We all went out front of the cabin with Buck with him leading the way towards an old locust tree near the barn. " Right here Lucas, look". Buck said as he pointed at a feather wedged onto the tree, it was a tail feather from a Red Hawk. Daisy then yelled out " I told you Lucas, you see, the scout put it there, why do you suppose he did that". Along with the other two I also stood there in amazement over the feather that was placed into the fork of the tree.

Buck already knew the story about the Red Hawk and when finding a single feather from his tail will always point you the way of your journey, but I saw I needed to explain the best I could to Daisy, being someone from back east and probably thinking all of this was superstition.

After trying to explain about the red feather, Daisy still seemed a little puzzled, but at the same time nodding her head like she understood what I had to say. But I'm sure if she stayed out west long enough she will start to understand. I told Buck and Daisy the night was getting cold and we need to get inside around some fire and maybe even cook up some grub. Buck said, " after this long day it doesn't matter if its grub or a grub worm, so long as I can get some shut eye afterwards". I couldn't have agreed more as we headed towards the cabin. I stopped on the porch to gather some firewood and told Buck and Daisy that I would be inside directly after gathering wood. Once they were inside I needed to stop what I was doing and ask the Lord for guidance on the journey ahead and may the Great Spirit continue to send us the signs which he did tonight. Even a tuff ole cowboy such as myself needs to have extra help every now and then or better yet, everyday.

After having some beans, and biscuits, I needed to ask Daisy a few more things so I said to her, " Tomorrow Buck and I need to ride on northward, but what are your plans"? Daisy told us that she needs to stay here at Broken Wheel, because there have been no answers as far as Miss Lora, " I mean I don't know if she left on her own, taken by someone or maybe even left just for a while getting supplies, I just don't know, but for sure I am not going anywhere until she comes back".

Being concerned for her safety I offered that she could come along with us, but straight out letting her know that the journey ahead could be a rough one and we will be coming across some renegade Cheyenne. Being the eastern girl she is, I don't think this idea had a lot of appeal to her so she replied, "I thank you for the offer Lucas, but I believe I need to stay here and wait for Lora". Of course I knew that was going to be her answer, and for that I was really glad, cause if I were in her shoes, I wouldn't have wanted to go either.

The next morning after seeing the sunrise and mostly clear skies all around, it brought me hope and anticipation of the trail ahead. I knew that the Platte river was still a day and a half ride ahead of us, but maybe along the trail we will come across something that will tell us why Tall Bull left our expedition or even anything at all with signs of Little Owls whereabouts. After getting up long before the others I already had some coffee ready then I grabbed a skillet and started hitting it with a spoon and yelling out, "get up we are wasting saddle time". Buck jumped up wondering where the gunshots came from and Daisy just about hit her head on the ceiling.

I really didn't have to say anything else, I just went outside and over to the barn to get our horses ready for the trip. While walking over there I did notice that the full moon was creating a bright shine on the tree where the feather was placed into its fork. Something like this may be nothing to others but to me I saw it as a confirmation that we are on the right track. So I got my horse saddled and even saddled Bucks horse, then took them over to the cabin and tied them to the post out front.

I went inside and told Buck that everything is ready to go and asked Daisy if it would be ok if we put a few rations in our saddle bags, maybe a couple of days worth. She said there is plenty here for her and to take anything we need because the food and water here is more than enough. So with us ready to hit the trail we thanked Daisy for letting us stay and tried to assure her that Miss Lora would soon be back. I didn't know what more we could say or do as far as Daisy and her survival here at Broken Wheel goes, but I had this strong feeling that she would be safe and sound where she is. After all if the Great Spirit led us to her, then why would he not help her also. Things like Daisy meeting up with Tall Bull and then Buck and I coming across Daisy aint just a matter of coindidence, it's a part of life's circle. And I am as sure as ever that by the end of this journey that circle will connect.

Next morning Buck and I hit the trail heading north out of Broken Wheel with the morning light to our east and a cloud of dust to our back. Buck hollered over to me "You reckon she will be alright Lucas", "She's a tough ole gal Buck, she will be just fine", I yelled back. I believe most of the morning we rode hard and steady with only a few stops for rest. We were starting to get into taller grass and rolling hills which meant the Platte River wasn't that far away, yet still a few more hours to go. Within a short time I saw a pair of cedar trees on top of a rise not far ahead and according to my memory once we get to those trees we should be able to see the Platte river. Which also means we aint far from where Little Owl was taken.

I was sure in hopes that before we got this far we would be able to find Tall Bull somewhere along the trail. But as we were approaching the pair of cedars I knew the chances of that happening was very slim. We started to slow down and approach the hill a little slower. I told Buck that the trees on the hill is where we need to be, because from there we can see the whole in all directions before we get to the river below. As we rode closer to the top of the ridge with its outline lowering ever so slowly showing us more of the land beyond its horizon, we started to become more alert, looking in all directions. Within a few yards of the cedar trees we dismounted and walked the rest of the way up then tied our horses to the tree.

Laying on the tall grass looking onward with our eye glasses moving from left to right trying to see anything at all. We laid there for the longest time asking each other if we see anything or not. Then finally I told Buck "Lets just ride on down there and see if maybe there are some tracks or any signs at all". So we climbed back on the saddle and rode down towards the river. This sure felt awfully risky cause if anyone was down there the river willows would keep them well hidden.

To our left was a low area going down to the river so we took it so we couldn't be seen in case there were someone along the river. About half way down we came across a bison skull laying in our pathway, and usually this is a common site but this skull was not common at all, because attached to it was a single feather, in fact a tail feather from a red tailed Hawk. Buck and I stopped as soon as we saw the skull, then I dismounted and walked over to the skull taking the feather from its grasp. Just as soon as I held the feather in my hand memories of the journey up to now and then visions of what is to come filled my head. All I could see were visions of riding this trail, the river beyond us, and several horses on the horizon with Tall Bull leading them on a white stallion. Then just as quick as these visions came they left when I heard Buck say "Lucas, you alright, what's wrong". I didn't want to tell him I was having visions about something, so all I told him was that I was just fine and only thinking , as I slid the feather into my vest pocket.

I climbed back up on my horse and told Buck that we need go straight down this draw till we reach the bank of the river. Buck was looking at me very curiously so he told me "Lucas, sometimes you sure get me wondering what's going on in your head, but for now you know the trail better than I do, so lets get after it". As we rode down the draw I kept thinking about the visions I was having and trying to figure out what they might have meant. I have always felt that even though the Lakota blood flowing through me was only half as my brothers, the Great Spirit was still with me as much as he was with them. We were coming upon a bend in this little draw so we proceeded slower and more cautious incase anybody or anything was around the corner. As we rounded the bend it looked as if we are still the only two men out here on the prairie. Within a few moments we were looking at the Platte river steady and calm with its tall Cottonwood and willows outlining its banks from east to west.

When we rode to the waters edge we dismounted and let our horses get a drink and we could also throw some water on our hot and dusty faces. Even though we had rode this long distance to find a lost brother, the cool and calming waters of the Platte seemed to give us a refreshing and keener look towards what might be next. As we left our horses standing in the water Buck and I walked further upon the bank looking up and down the river trying to see anything that might seem like someone has been here. My eyes were drawn to a small willow tree which stretched out over the water. I saw something shining in the tree where it met the waters edge, so I walked over to see just what it was. I reached down and pulled it up from the water and saw it was a trap, not just a common trap, but a Lakota trap. I yelled over to Buck who was searching the banks ahead of me, "Buck, come over here, I found one of

Tall Bulls traps". Buck quickly came over and took the trap from my hands, looking at it for the longest time then asked me, "Are you sure this is a Lakota trap"? I told him that without a doubt this was not only Lakota but it was Tall Bulls trap because I have been with him before when he used them.

We figured that if I went downstream a couple hundred yards and Buck went upstream about the same we would be able to find a dead critter that Tall Bull and Little Owl had set their traps out for. So we began searching the banks with Buck heading east and me heading west. So far I wasn't having any luck finding signs of anyone that may have been along the rivers edge or even further upon its banks, other than this one trap. So I turned back around to go see if Buck found anything. I yelled out for him stood there in silence for a moment and heard no response. So I went back over to my horse and rode a little ways further then yelled out to him again, and still no response. Then finally a few seconds later I heard Buck yell out, "Over here Lucas". He had gone a little further up the bank and found where several horses had made a path going up the dirt bank and headed north.

I remember Tall Bull telling me they couldn't find any of their traps when he and Little Owl set out searching for them. So why have we found one at the base of this willow and one of the best trappers around like Tall Bull saw nothing. I looked over to Buck and told him that something is not right here and we should ride further up river then take the western trail which leads to Cheyenne territory. We both agreed that this was the best answer in trying to find Little Owl especially after hearing Tall Bulls story about when they were here at the river. We found a crossing further up and went for it as quick as we could with water flying in all directions and our horses keeping their heads high. Once we were on the other side we took off northwest with our hats blowing back and the water blowing off our horses mane, showering us for at least a mile.

We rode hard and steady hoping that just over the next rise would be the answer to this entire journey and then everything would be alright. But as all the rises came and passed we started feeling as if we were never going to see any signs of life on this trail. About the time I was thinking there was nothing out here we both stopped at the same time and pulled our rifles out from the saddle sheath. On the ridge ahead there were at a least two dozen horses and their riders. From this distance I couldn't see who they were, but I will bet ya they were Cheyenne for sure. I looked over to Buck and said "Dang Buck, looks like we either run back or go up and tell them why we are here". Buck and I have never been ones to run away from anything, so Buck tells me, "Lucas, lets ride on up to there and you do all the talking, cause you know Cheyenne better than I do, and just right out ask them where the heck is Little Owl". Buck was right, we really didn't have any other choice other than turn and run, and that would only make us look like cowards in their eyes. At least this way it shows bravery from us and hopefully respect from them. But if they are the renegades, forget it, we are both dead men.

We put our rifles back but made sure our side arms were free and ready. We then slowly started riding towards the ridge lined with Cheyenne. At the same time the whole line of riders on the ridge started their approach towards us, then as we came closer to them I saw that they were Cheyenne, and they were not the renegades that Tall Bull remembered, because leading them was Chief Standing Bear and I remember him from years ago. I told Buck as we rode closer, "There is nothing to worry about, I know the chief, he is called Standing Bear, I met him a few years back near Laramie, and hopefully he will remember me". The Cheyenne stopped just short a dozen yards from us forming a half circle around Buck and I. Neither of us moved for a few moments then I nudged my horse taking a few steps closer to the chief and he did the same.

With the normal greetings out of the way I then told Standing Bear who we were and why we were there, with no other reason than to find my brothers Little Owl and Tall Bull. Standing Bear sat tall on his horse looking at me straight in the eye, he had no expression on his face, not even a blink of his eye. Then he said to me "Lucas Clay, I remember you". I told him of our meeting near Laramie a few years back and he nodded his head agreeing that is where he remembered me. So then I asked him "Standing Bear, can you tell me anything about the whereabouts of my brothers"? He told me he knew of these Lakota men but hasn't seen anyone until they saw us. He also told me they were in search of some braves that broke away from the tribe because they were being led by Grey Wolf, and that he has been on several raids throughout this land and they have set out to find and stop him or else there will be war within their nation and for sure with the whites. Standing Bear then told me "You shall go in peace now Lucas Clay". He motioned to the rest of his braves and they all turned and rode away.

As the Cheyenne rode off on their quest to find Grey Wolf and his band, I started thinking if they are tracking the renegades, and Little Owl may have been taken by them, then we should go in their direction. I turned back towards Buck and told him my idea about following the Cheyenne. We both agreed that following them would get us to Little Owl quicker than on our own, but to follow them would sure be risky, we would have to track them at least a half a day behind. With time being either our enemy or friend we chose to ride up to the ridge where we first saw Standing Bear and his braves. It would be from that point we could see them for several miles and know the direction of their travel.

While on the ridge letting our horses graze we were going over in our heads the past several days trying to come up with an answer as to why Tall Bull left our camp, but still would place the red feathers for us to follow. Then one other small detail was the lone trap I found back at the river, which may have no meaning at all, but it still has stuck in my crawl. Buck finally said to me "Lucas, I don't know what all these things mean, but I do know that you are the one that will be given the answer, not me, you are the one Tall Bull came to needing help to find Little Owl not me, but as your friend I am here to help you and by darn that is what I am going to do". I told him " I reckon your right Buck, this journey will either redeem me or bury me, but as far as me having all the answers, I wouldn't stake your life on it, besides if you have any ideas I would expect you to share them".

I began walking around to stretch my legs and think about our next move. I knew from here we would follow the path the Cheyenne were taking but I needed more than just following Standing Bear. I needed the instincts of my Lakota roots, I needed to start thinking the way they think. No harm has come to us so far, even with a few set backs, we are still on the right trail. I know one thing for sure, and that's if the Great Spirit wasn't riding with us we would have bit the dust a long time ago.

We waited on the ridge several hours for the Cheyenne to be so far ahead of us they wouldn't be able to tell there was someone tracking them. Because if they were to find out then Buck and I would be dead men for sure. I know first hand that these people don't cotton to being followed and for sure they will have the last word, and yours doesn't count. We felt pretty safe by now because we have been waiting around here for about six hours and so we agreed that now is the time to follow their trail. We took off in their direction but after a few hours had passed we needed to rely on their signs of travel. To me tracking anything out here in the flatlands is like tracking buffalo in the snow, they leave a map as to where they are going and even why they did.

I could tell we were starting to gain on them a little, so every now and then we would stop to rest and try to come up with some ideas about how to approach the two bands of Cheyenne when and if we ride upon them. This is going to be the biggest challenge when we get to the point of no return. That point is when Standing Bear confronts Grey

Wolf and we find that Little Owl is being held by them. After hitting the trail again I saw a few trees to our left and yelled over to Buck pointing to the trees, " Lets go over there". He nodded his head and we rode over to a little tree grove not just for a resting place, but to help hide us as well cause I knew we were getting closer to the Cheyenne and didn't want to be seen in case a couple of the braves where scouting around for the main band.

As we brought our horses in around this little group of cedar trees we were starting to realize that the moment of truth is coming very shortly. I told Buck that even though its getting closer to sundown, I believe Standing Bear already knows where Grey Wolf has his encampment, and if Little Owl is being held there, then somehow we need to get him out of there before trouble starts, because Grey Wolf just might use Little Owl to save his own hide.

I was once told a story from an old Confederate soldier that happen to be passing through the valley and stopped at my ranch on the Greenhorn for some water and food. We were standing by my corrals while his horse was watering and we were just talking about different things along his trail so I asked him what brings him this direction. He started telling me about the Langston Creek battle back in Tennessee when he and his best friend Henry whom he had been best friends with since childhood were separated during the battle. He said there was no family to speak of just Henry. So he started running through the smoke filled creek bottom with artillery fire all around then finally making his way up to higher ground. While looking off beyond the other side of the creek the smoke started to clear and he saw Henry running up the hill firing his pistol and yelling. He told me he ran out in to the open to get Henrys attention then that's all he could remember. He came too several days later in a field hospital with wounds to his shoulder and legs.

I asked the ole man whose name was Clyde, "So why does that bring you all the way here"? He told me the war ended not long after that battle so he went in search of Henry. He found that what was left of Henrys family had moved out west to Durango thinking Henry didn't survive. Clyde looked at me with determination in his eyes and said, " So you see Lucas, I have been through hell and back, yet family has always been a guiding light for me no matter how far I travel or face trouble along the way, I will find Henry who has always been like a brother to me.

As I sat here looking off into the distance remembering this ole man and his quest for being re-united with his family, I believe there aint much difference between what he was doing and what Buck and I are doing right now. I have many friends back home and one of them is riding with me, but when it comes to family, well most are all gone, but I still have my Lakota brothers.

Knowing what has to be done I told Buck we need to get to Grey Wolfs camp before Standing Bear does and find a place where we can see if Little Owl is there. Then once we see where he is being held, we will wait till after nightfall when there camp is silent then go to Little Owl and bring him back to our horses. Buck told me that would be very risky for only the two of us. "Buck", I said, "There was a time when either one of us would tackle this on our own, so with the two of us we should have a better chance". We saddled back up and rode towards the trail which Standing Bear laid behind then followed instincts and circled further out and then back hoping to see or smell smoke from Grey Wolfs camp.

Nightfall was going to be upon us very soon and we needed to find the camp and some sort of a look-out spot before it became to dark to see anything. Then as luck would have it a slight breeze started to come in from the north, then Buck, who was riding a few yards ahead of me stopped and waved for me to catch up to him. He had his head tilted back and asked me, "Can you smell that? It sure smells like smoke to me". And sure enough I could also smell smoke, that breeze brought it in and the campfire from it couldn't be any more than a mile away. We took off northward in its direction and the smoke smell started getting a little stronger. No further than a half mile we could see smoke coming from a small valley ahead. We knew this had to be Grey Wolfs camp so we rode just a little further to get a good view of the area. Not to take any more chances than we had to we stopped to look around for a spot ahead that could serve as a lookout towards the camp. There was a large rock outcropping just off to the east of the camp where we would be able to see the area and be well hidden. Once we got to the rocks we tied our horses to some scrubs and climbed on up to take a look at the camp through our eye glasses. And by golly it was Grey Wolfs camp alright and luckily no sign of Standing Bear. I was just surprised that we were able to circle back in and get here before Standing Bear did.

We laid on the edge of the rocks watching every move down at that camp and further out for any braves walking the area. We were able to see four of them about a hundred yards out from the center of camp in all four directions, but only one of them would need to be silenced. Then Buck tapped my arm and said, "Lucas, look to the far left of camp, I see a man up against a tree with a brave sitting in front of him". Trying to look through these glasses with the sun going down I just couldn't make out who it was or what they were doing. I told Buck "wait here I will be right back, I need to go down a little further to see who is against the tree". I headed down the hill as low as possible and stopped at a sage brush looking through my glasses at the man against the tree. It was Little Owl with a brave sitting on the ground not far from him as a guard. Slowly I went back to the rocks to tell Buck what I saw.

I told Buck that not only do we need to take care of the outer guard but also the one standing guard in front of Little Owl. Buck told me "I don't think Little Owl would recognize me very quickly so what if you went down towards camp and I took care of the brave on the south edge"? Giving it only a couple seconds of thought I knew his suggestion was how it needed to be. I knew Buck was very capable of taking care of the guard with complete surprise and no sound at all. Then with some good timing I would do the same for the one standing guard before Little Owl. Buck gave me plenty of time to go further down hill towards the Cheyenne's camp and take position not to far away from Little Owl and the brave guarding him.

With every ounce of survival blood I had within me, I was moving across the ground like a cat sneaking up on a mouse. As I was crawling closer I had to keep my eyes on the guard and all the little twigs laying around so I wouldn't break one and have the brave come and check out the noise. So far I have made it within a few yards of the tree then laid very still waiting for the right time to make my move.

I saw the guard was getting restless stretching his arms and looking around so now was the time to get even closer to him. Just as soon as he stretched again, I jumped over to him cupping my hand around his mouth to keep him silent and my arm around his neck. I had no intentions of killing him, but only forcing him to pass out. Once he became limp I hog tied him and placed a gag around his mouth. I turned around towards Little Owl and his eyes were as big as dollars. I went over to him and cut the ropes from around the tree which had him bound then without saying anything I motioned for him to follow me. We both left the camp area just as quiet as I came in and not leaving any trace of our direction at all.

We finally came to the rocks to meet up with Buck and hopefully he had no problem with the other brave. We climbed to the top and there was Buck looking through the glasses making sure there was no one stirring around because of us taking Little Owl. This whole time coming up the hill neither of us said a single word to each other, but now that we were further away and felt safer Little Owl looked at me and said "Lucas, how did you know"? I told him "Tall Bull had come to me at the ranch and told me the story about the two of you checking traps, then you had disappeared, so we took off to search for you, but within a short time on the trail Tall Bull left us to go on his own, but I believe he left red feathers to show us the way". I told Little Owl that the journey to find him will be a story he can tell around the fire, but for now we need to get him home. Little Owls eyes were wide open and had such a shocked look on his face. He grabbed my arm and started to tell me something when we heard loud voices from the camp below. I interrupted and told him we needed to go now. I told Buck to go due east and Little Owl will ride with him, cause I was going to stay a good distance behind to keep an eye out for any one that may find our trail. By sunrise we should be far enough away there will be no chance of them catching up.

Buck and Little Owl took off eastward while I stayed behind giving them at least a half hour ride ahead of me. This way I can stay here on the rocks keeping watch over the camp and hopefully see what all the yelling was about. A full moon sure would have helped but tonight was a cool windy night with the clouds moving to where every now and then you could see an opening with stars and a small slice of the moon. It just wasn't enough for me to get a good look at anything below. As I sit here in the night thinking about this entire journey from the time Tall Bull arrived at the ranch and our ride northward to find Little Owl my thoughts started to ask questions such as, why have I not come upon

Tall Bull? where did Miss Lora go? where is Standing Bear this whole time? Right now is a perfect time for the Great Spirit to give me a few helpful hints.

I wasn't hearing anymore yelling from the camp so by now I figured enough time had passed that I should saddle up and head out east behind Buck and Little Owl. But to make sure I climbed up one rock higher to take another look towards Grey Wolfs camp. I saw some movement around the campfire and some more around the edges of the fire light. I tried to focus in on the area where I found Little Owl tied to a tree but it was to dark at this time to see anything further out from the fire. Something was going on down in there and I knew it had to be that they found out Little Owl was gone when the brave I had tied and gagged was discovered. I tried my best to see anything through these glasses yet also trying my best to stay out of anyone's site.

I knew with all the movement at the camp I needed to stay put for a while so I could keep a watch on them in case they found any signs of my departure with Little Owl. Then just as soon as some clouds started moving away the moon brightened up the path which Little Owl and I took coming up to these rocks. I saw at least three braves making their way up the hill coming straight at me.

I couldn't go down to my horse and try to catch up to Buck cause then they would catch up to all three of us for sure. But with only two or three of them I felt I had a better chance of taking each of them out one at a time as they started climbing around the rocks. I left my gear on top then started to crawl down to a split in the rocks and stay there until one of them passed in front of me. Within a few seconds one came within a couple of feet, so I reached out to him with both arms around his neck and with a slight twist he fell into the opening where I hid. I eased my way out of the rocks crawling as slow and silent as possible in search of the others. I realized I needed to make my way back up to the top where I left my gear cause I didn't want them to find any trace of where we were going or how many of us there are. All they should come across is find-ing one brave tied up and Little Owl gone.

At a turtles crawl I started making my way back to the top of the rocks without out making the slightest noise. I knew there were still two more Cheyenne braves out here in the dark looking for someone and right now that someone is me. As I became nearer to the top I started to see some of my gear, so at least I knew they didn't find any of that. When I reached the top of the rock I turned around checking the area below and I was surprised by a brave standing be-fore me with a tomahawk in the air. Still lying on my back looking up at him I managed to roll to one side as he swung his weapon down towards me missing me within an inch. I grabbed his hatchet then during the struggle I flipped him over the side of the rocks knowing he couldn't survive a fall of that distance. The other brave came running up towards me, but with the hatchet still in my hand I threw it his way and sent him falling down the path from which he came. I quickly ran down to my horse and took off as fast as ole Ruger could take me because the rest of the band are going to come looking for the those three braves and when they find them, a war party is coming.

Not long after leaving those rocks the land started to become more flat and grassy and even in the dark of night I was able to make out an outline of the eastern horizon far ahead. In hopes to slow down anyone trying to track me I would ride a straight line and then go off to one side or the other for a short distance. I knew if I could ride at this pace with no trouble ahead or behind me I would be able to catch up to Buck within a couple of hours. Ever so often I would stop for a breather and look back to the west making sure I wasn't being followed, and so far I have been in the clear.

I figured that somewhere ahead Buck and Little Owl would stop for most of the night because of riding double. My only concern right now was missing them for a small distance and passing them altogether. I could see a small tree ahead so I thought I had better stop there and let Ruger rest and me also. I poured some of my water from the canteen into my hat and let him have a well deserved drink then let him eat some grass while I got my focus on the rest of the ride ahead. I started walking around the area hoping to find some tracks but it wasn't that easy in the night. I knew when it came to night riding that Buck would also pick the brightest star in the direction he was going and follow it, and that's exactly what I was doing.

I was making my way back over to my horse after looking for any tracks when I saw something hanging on a branch of the tree. The closer I got it seemed to shimmer back and forth like it was going to blow away. I reached out and grabbed the limb then took hold of the object thinking what it probably was. Then looking at it closer I saw it was a red feather, one from a Red Tailed Hawk. I don't understand how this could be, how Tall Bull would know where to place a feather out here in the middle of a wide prairie, in fact I could have rode further in either direction and then stopped. At this point I knew that this journey meant more that just rescuing Little Owl.

I sat on the ground with my back against the tree holding the feather and thinking about all the possible events which could happen on the trail ahead. The worst one would be if Grey Wolf and his band where to catch up to us before we reached the Lakota territory. But chances are that Standing Bear will meet up with him long before they even think about coming our way. I went over and placed the feather in my saddle bags along with the others, saddled up and took off to find Buck and Little Owl. I knew it couldn't be that much further till I came within yards of them because so far the red feathers haven't led us astray yet. The clouds opened up all the sudden to where I could see more of the area because of the moonlight, so at a slow walk I was able to see a rise ahead of me with a grove of trees and I knew that was where Buck would be. So I rode that direction at a slow pace till coming within a hundred feet or so then called out "Hello in the camp". I didn't know if anyone was there or not so I called out one more time and waited in silence, then I heard my name being called out, "Lucas, is that you, Lucas". I knew that voice and I called back, "Yes Buck its me, I'm coming in".

As I rode closer I saw his horse tied to a tree and then saw Buck and Little Owl standing not far away, I climbed down and walked on over to them. With a firm hand shake from both of them and awfully glad to see them I started telling what had happened after they had left our rocky lookout back at Grey Wolfs camp. Little Owls first thought was that they would be right behind me and we needed to leave now. I told them I was very careful trying to throw them off with my tracks and have stopped and watched ever so often my entire ride to make sure it were clear behind me, but also admitting the Cheyenne are pretty good trackers even at night. But with me needing to silence three of the Cheyenne braves we did agree that getting back on the trail was something that needed to happen right away or the same thing will happen to us.

Buck told me they had been at this spot for about an hour hoping I would get there pretty darn quick or they would have to keep riding on, but no sooner than he started to talk again Little Owl motioned for us to keep silent while looking off in the distance. He looked at us and quietly said, "Horses coming, slowly, but they are there". I told Buck to go over to our horses, and Little Owl and I would go a little further out and wait. We laid in the grass about twenty feet from each other watching the moonlit prairie for any riders. I was able to focus on two horses and their riders approaching us, so I knew Little Owl had seen them also. This is no time to ask questions or to welcome anyone, cause chances are they were scouting braves with Grey Wolf.

I was sure Little Owl was thinking the same thing I was, then as they became closer we would jump them at the same time. Then just as soon as the rider closer to me came within distance I jumped up from the grass ramming the horse in the lower part of the neck causing him to raise up then fall over. Just as soon as he fell I pinned the stunned brave to the ground and silenced him with his own knife. I quickly grabbed his horse then searched the dim moonlit area looking for Little Owl. I saw a horse not far from me and called out, "Little Owl, you ok". And to my relief he answered back, "I am ok Lucas".

It was just as I had thought, these were two Cheyenne scouts from Grey Wolfs band, they had tracked me at night all the way from there camp. No matter how careful a man can be when trying to cover his trail, or how silent you believe you are, these men who know every blade of grass in prairie will instantly find that needle in a hay stack. We grabbed the ropes of the two braves horses and went back over where Buck was waiting. When he saw the two Cheyenne horses he said, "Well great, they are really gonna be mad now, but at least that's five down and who knows how many to go". So with those words of wisdom we got the heck out of there and with Little Owl riding his own horse, we should travel quickly.

It shouldn't be that long before a dim eastern light will show us the beginning of Lakota territory, the first ridges of the Black Hills. With this anticipation before us and the possibility of Grey Wolf not far behind the three of us rode like lightning across the sky. We finally came upon Bitter Creek and started crossing its water feeling such relief that we had made it to are destination. But not all is safe until we know if we have been followed or not. We went to the first plateau on the other side so we can see in most all directions around us. Waiting and watching, the sky became brighter with the rising sun and we were able to see for miles to the west and saw no signs of anyone following us. Little Owl rode further ahead while Buck and I stayed put watching for anything in the distance. I asked Buck "Did you say anything to Little Owl about Tall Bull, cause we sure didn't have time to talk about it before". He told me the riding was hard and long and they said hardly anything at all, even when they stopped waiting for me.

I could still see Little Owl as he rode off towards the north scouting for anyone who could have been around. Then looking back west again there seemed to be a slight cloud of dust a few miles away. I told Buck to look in his eyeglasses and see what he makes of it. We knew this was not an early morning ground fog, it had to be dust from several running horses. We didn't dare signal for Little Owl, we only moved our horses to a little lower ground and kept watch towards the dust. As the figures of horses started to come within view and the dust behind them we were able to see that it was no doubt Grey Wolfs band of renegades coming towards us following the exact path we took. Then Buck grabbed me on the shoulder saying, "Dad gum it Lucas, look over to south, some more riders are coming this way". I told him Grey Wolf does not have that many braves so its either Standing Bear or the Army, cause they are both looking for him.

We seemed to be caught in the middle of a dog gone battlefield and half of them want our hides. Something big is going to take place and I cant be sure if they know we're here or not. And now I'm not able to see Little Owl anymore so I sure hope he is able to see what Buck and I are watching in the distance. I guess they know we are here cause our trouble has just started. We both heard what we thought were our horses behind us but only to turn and see four Cheyenne renegades on their horses standing there. As Buck and I stood up very slowly I told him I would tell them we were trappers looking for small furs. This didn't seem to be the right explanation cause three of them jumped off their horses and tackled Buck and I to the ground. The other one stayed on his horse with his bow in hand and an arrow pointing our way. He began moving closer till I was able to smell the scent from his horses leg. I told Buck not to make any moves at all and for sure don't look up at him. I heard one of them say "Tie these white men up, Grey Wolf will want to deal with them his way".

I could feel the sharp point of their spear holding me to the ground, expecting it to sink deeper into my flesh, but instead they pulled us up and tied Buck and I together back to back still sitting on the ground. Knowing their ways I knew this was going to be Bucks and mine final hours cause here we are hog tied by four Cheyenne renegades and more of them riding closer. Then all the sudden the brave that remained on his horse called to the others, "leave them here for now, lets go back and tell Grey Wolf". They rode back south leaving us tied like calves during branding time. We tried everything to get ourselves free but nothing seemed to be working. Then all of the sudden out of nowhere we saw a man walking towards us saying," remain still and I will cut you free", the man said. As he came closer we saw it was Tall Bull, standing in front of us with his knife ready to cut our ropes.

Tall Bull reached between us and with one swift cut the ropes fell to the ground. We stood up and I started asking, "where in world have you been and how did you get passed that bunch out there'? I had a few more questions but Tall Bull stopped me before I got them out and said, "Lucas, soon you will see the battle between good and bad, our people have tried to keep our lands safe and our children strong so they may grow and continue the circle of life which the Great Spirit has given us.

Grey Wolf and his braves chose to turn there backs on us by raiding the whites and putting the rest of our people in danger. Lucas, my brother, today you have been given a choice, remember the red feather led you here, and it has always lead us to the right path".

As soon as Tall Bull told me this we heard a horse riding upon us then turned to see who it was. It was Little Owl coming back like the wind and barley getting his horse stopped at our feet. He jumped down and immediately told us about Grey Wolf's position and it was for sure Standing Bear coming from the other direction. I told Little Owl that Tall Bull was just telling us about the battle that he believes is about to take place. Little Owl just stood there looking puzzled and glancing around to see if anyone else were here. I turned to tell Tall Bull to explain what he had just told us, but he wasn't there. As Little Owl moved closer he placed his hand on my shoulder and said, "Lucas if the Great Spirit has spoken to you that is a good, but it was not Tall Bull that told you these things, and if it were him then you have seen a vision. Lucas, Tall Bull was killed last winter when Grey Wolf first resisted Chief Standing Bear. Then Buck spoke out and said, " that cant be so cause he was with us at the beginning of our ride and even though he disappeared for a while, he was here just know". Little Owl replied, "Because you are friend on the same journey you have shared the same vision, but Lucas I thought you received word about Tall Bull, I am sorry".

If it were only me I would toss it up as perhaps getting older and my memory is fading, or even in the saddle too long, but in this case Buck has been with me this entire time seeing and hearing everything I have, even Miss Daisy talked to him. Instead of standing here all day trying to put this together I told Buck and Little Owl we need to make a move cause Grey Wolf by now knows we are here. Then Little Owl spoke up and said, "I am going to meet Standing Bear, he is chief of my people and I must fight with him." He then jumped back onto his horse and rode off towards Standing Bear as fast as he could. I looked at Buck and told him, "You heard Tall Bull when he told me I had a choice to make, and I know now what he meant, we either stay here which we will die for sure, we run to the east like scared rabbits, or I fight for the future of my brothers.

Well ole Buck stood in front of me looking me square in the eyes and said, "Lucas Clay you have been my friend more years than I can count, we have seen the good and the bad thrown at us and always came out alive and well, so what ever you decide right now is alright with me, but let me say this, you have never seen me run away nor have you ever seen me turn down a good fight."

Hearing this I knew what my choice was, I knew why the Great Spirit had sent Tall Bull, to show me my way of redemption. These are the people of my grandmother whose blood still flows through me. If I could not make a difference here today, then I believe Tall Bull would not have come to me. So I replied to Buck, "I am going down to meet up with Little Owl and chief Standing Bear, I will be honored that you will fight with me." We started making sure that every gun we had was fully loaded and more ammo was within reach. Without saying a word we mounted our horses, looked at each other and with a simple nod we rode down the hill our hats blowing back and rifles raised and ready.

The battle had already begun so we rode straight towards Grey Wolf and his band of renegades with our Winchesters at eye level picking our targets. After my vision of Tall Bull I knew the Great Spirit had led me to this moment, so with him at my side I was riding straight into the enemy feeling like I had the sight of an eagle and the strength of a buffalo while firing my rifle and using its stock as a club. I was able to see Buck off to my right standing in his stirrups with his rifle in one hand and his pistol in the other just ah yelling and cussing like a wild man.

I was able to see Little Owl riding through the enemy shooting off more arrows than one could count. I saw Standing Bear holding the front line like a bull buffalo protecting his herd. All the while fighting my way through a mass of horses and angry men fighting and yelling their war cries. I made my way to the outer edge of the battle looking for an entry on my return, then I saw Buck riding towards me. As he came closer I noticed a lone figure on horseback behind Buck on the plateau which we had come from and I knew who it was. So when Buck came along beside me I looked over again and he was gone. I yelled out to Buck "this is our day Buck, lets show um just what we're made of".

Today my life had taken hold of its roots and witnessed the struggle between good and bad while conquering its enemies within a single battle. As Tall Bull once told me, "you must know your heart first then you will truly live for tomorrow.

BISHOP'S GOLD

THE HIDDEN TREASURE

BY
ROD SHAHAN

CHAPTER 4

Bishop's Gold

The Hidden Treasure

THERE AIN'T VERY many people that this ole cow-poke doesn't take a liken to when I'm out on the trail or even going into town for supplies cause that's when you are sure to meet some one new every time, whether in the general store or maybe they are just riding into town. But I'll be dog gone if I didn't meet one of those rare people just the other day in front of the local Assay office. The only reason I was there was because my cousin Greg ran the office and not cause I had any claims anywhere, I just like stopping in sometimes and talking over ole times with him and looking at any new pictures he has drawn up, cause this boy is one heck of an artist.

Anyway just as soon as I dismounted and began to put my horses leather to the hitchin post I was almost knocked down to the ground when Ruger comes swinging over to me yelling like a coyote. I grabbed hold of the post and was ready to chew Ruger out when I looked over and saw this huge mule next to us with a ton of tools along with pots and pans hanging on him. Then I heard this voice ring out "Move over fellow, this aint no personal hitchin post ya know". I came out from around my horse with my fist tight and turning white. I went to the other side of that mule ready for a fight, that is until I saw this old prospector standing before me with a lifetime of anguish and determination on his face. He looked straight up at me with his shoulders back and his chin forward then simply said "WHAT".

Mind ya now, I am not one to make an enemy out of anyone, let alone a stranger whom I know nothing about, but the temptation for doing that was certainly within reach. So I told the old man, "Sorry, my name is Lucas, I apologize for us pushing you over, and who might you be". He looked me and my horse over with a certain amount of curiosity and replied " I am Jefferson Bishop, and I am here to make a claim in your assay office, got any objections to that young fellow".

Well, his name was certainly worth a good amount of respect even if the man was hard to know. But I always figured that just about anybody was worth the benefit of the doubt no matter how cranky they seemed. I walked on over to the office door holding it open a little bit longer so that Mr Bishop could walk on in, but I reckon that wasn't the thing to do either. He scolded me by saying "Get on in there, do I look like some woman to you, now go". Ok, so that's mistake number two, so I guess I'll quite with the niceness now and get on with why I am even here.

As I walked on into the Assay office I saw my cousin Greg sitting behind his desk working away on his daily business, that is until I got a little closer and saw that he was sketching out some pictures. Before Mr. Bishop could say anything I told Greg " I met this man outside just now and his name is Jefferson Bishop, so Greg if you don't mind, I will just sit over here and mind my own business while you two carry on with yours". With that being said I waited for some kind of response, like, no, you wait outside, or even, your right it is none of your business. But that never happened, so I sat there patiently while they went over Mr. Bishops claim business.

Sitting there trying to read a few wanted posters and anything else laying around I still couldn't help but hear some of what the talking was all about. So here is the jest of it. It seems Mr. Bishop happened into a piece of ground further up the Greenhorn and wants to officially lay claim on anything it has. And then Greg keeps wanting some sort of proof that he can do it legally. So with Greg looking through his files and Mr. Bishop walking in and out bringing more papers he had in his saddle bags, it sounded as if they had everything figured out and was ready to call the transaction a done deal. And all I could think of was "Its about dog gone time cause I got some other business to take care of".

Gregg and Mr. Bishop stood up shaking hands, with Gregg telling him, "Now you be sure to come back in by the end of the week and I'll have the papers recorded and signed for you". Mr. Bishop didn't say anything more than, "I'll be here". As soon as he was out the door and headed down the street I turned to Gregg and asked him, "Ok cuz, where is that ole mans claim? And don't be telling me its personal either". Gregg told me to sit back down cause I wasn't going to like it much. He asked me if I recall that ole dugout that has been abandoned for several years just north a little ways from Badger Basin. "I sure do" I told him, "So is that his claim"? Gregg looked very reluctant to answer so I said it for him. "It is, and you know dog gone good and well that I graze my herd up there every year, and I have for almost ten years". Gregg said he couldn't do anything cause Mr. Bishop showed proof of ownership that his father gave to him and it took up about a hundred acres plus his mineral claim.

After a few minutes of thinking this over I realized that Jefferson Bishop was only confirming any claim that was rightfully his by way of his Dad, and that Gregg was only doing his job. Gregg said to me, "Lucas, I know you all to well and you have never caused trouble, you have either worked around it, or put an end to it, so what's it going to be in Mr. Bishops case"? "Well Gregg", I said, "I have no choice but to work around it and see if Mr. Bishop will let me continue to graze my cattle up there, but if not, I guess I'll just take them on down to the Ophir Creek valley". Gregg then gave a sigh of relief and told me if I needed any help bringing them down just say the word and he will be there. I told him " You bet I will be calling on you, but first I need to visit Mr. Bishop to see if a deal can be worked out so I can continue to graze up there every end of summer cause the grass seems to stay a little richer there than Ophir Creek.

My intentions this morning was to just stop by the assay office and talk a little bit like I often do, but this time it was a heck of lot different. I walked out of there with a whole new outlook on the next several months rather than looking at Greggs drawings and listening to family current events. Yep, by golly I stepped down from that boardwalk onto the street standing beside my horse looking this ole town of Greenhorn up one side and down the other. I looked over to Ruger and told him, " Well, ya know ole partner we only came into town for beans, flour and bacon, so lets go get it and head back home.

As I started walking over to the general store I heard this mighty awful scream mixed with a bunch of men yelling. Looking on down the street I saw Jefferson Bishops mule turning in circles screaming up a storm and then Jefferson trying to calm him down while cussing out the Lawson brothers, who were standing next to him yelling, laughing and waving their arms. The Lawson brothers are nothing but trouble around these parts so I ran down to help Jefferson with his mule and get rid of those brothers. As I got up there Mr. Bishop gave me the rope to his mule and yelled out, "hold onto my mule Lucas". Without thinking why, I held the mules rope while Jefferson went over to the Lawson brothers and like a tornado he had both of those boys face down on the ground with their arms behind their backs. I quickly tied his mule to hitchin post then held down one of the brothers till they decided to calm down. I guess they decided real quick that Jefferson Bishop isn't just some ole ordinary prospector cause they gave in quickly yelling out "Ok, Ok, we're sorry". As we let them up they resorted to their regular all bark and no bite selves by Clem Lawson saying as they cowardly walked away, " This aint the end of this ole man, and you should have minded your own business Lucas". I simply shook it off as a couple of town brats cause that's all I have ever known them to be.

Once Clem and Albert Lawson made their way

on down the street back towards the saloon I knew this wasn't going to be the end of this little fight cause several town folk were watching as the boys were taken down by an old prospector and an old cowboy. I have known these boys their whole lives. Their dad was hung as a horse thief when they were young and their mother worked day and night taking in laundry in order to support them. When their mother died three years ago with the fever those two boys simply turned mean and rebellious towards anyone around. I would like to say this is the end of that little feud with those two and it was only the whiskey talking. But knowing them like I do I reckon I had better not turn my back on them any more.

I handed the rope for Jeffersons mule over to him and apologized for the trouble he had right off the bat. I was a little surprised when he said to me, " Lucas, thank you for your help, but I really could have handled those two idiots myself". And from what I saw walking over there I knew he wasn't bragging. This ole man could have handled them and the rest of their family and friends. I told him it was ok and offered my help for any future needs he may have. Jefferson did tell me that he didn't know all that much about the lay of the land around his claim and asked if I knew the area up there. I saw this as my opportunity to not only help him with knowing the land but perhaps making a deal to keep my cattle grazing there for at least a couple more months.

"Why sure Mr. Bishop" I said," I know that area very well cause I have been grazing that area for several years, but I sure didn't know who the owner was until now, so it looks like we need to have a talk about me grazing on your land". I was expecting some sort of a rude comment but instead he told me to come up by the ole dug out tomorrow and we would talk about it. Then said, "By the way, don't tell anyone about my business today". I assured him that if anyone finds out it sure as heck didn't come from me.

Mr Bishop headed out of town and I felt a sense of relief that I may not have to move my cattle and at the same time just possibly made a new friend. Too bad that possible friendship had to start with putting down a couple of roughnecks like the Lawson boys. After getting the supplies I had needed and stuffing my saddle bags full, I noticed those two roughnecks were standing outside the saloon looking like they weren't done trying to cause more trouble. So I mounted up and rode down the street passing them within a few feet, the whole time feeling their mischievous stares. I rode no more than a few yards past them when one yelled out my name then I felt a rock hit me on the back. I immediately turned Ruger around and headed right into the two of them, knocking them both down onto the dusty street. They started cussing and trying to get up but I told Ruger, "keep um down boy". Ruger started shaking his head and raring up like he wanted to stomp a mud hole them. And those boys just started crawling faster and further away.

When I thought they had enough we backed off and let them get to their feet. As soon as Clem started to say something I gave Ruger a nudge and he knocked him back down again. So I asked Albert if he wanted to say anything. "No sir Mr. Clay" he replied, Albert being the youngest of the two hasn't had as many years to practice being mean as Clem has. I told the two of them that their mother would be turning over in her grave if she knew how they were turning out to be. " So now I am going to tell the both of you this only one time" I said to them, "In case you have any more idiot ideas about causing trouble with Mr. Bishop, just remember that he and I are friends. So that means if you cause trouble for him, you are causing trouble for me, and I sure hope you realize how that's going to end up". They both stood there looking up at me in silence till I nudged Ruger one more time then they quickly replied, "Yes sir Mr. Clay, no more trouble from us, we promise".

Riding out of town with that little episode still on my mind, and knowing those two like everyone else in town does, I am certain that by the end of the day they will be even more worked up. But I suppose one good thing will probably happen, they will be so drunk that by tomorrow they won't remember a thing. So I reckon I have more things to dwell on besides thinking about those two idiots. One thought for sure is going over to Jefferson Bishops place and talking to him about the grazing and seeing if he needs any help getting his new place fit to live in. Of course I'll need to approach that part very carefully because he seems to be a man that will do everything on his own no matter how bad the odds are. Holy cow, kinda sounds like me, so maybe this wont be so difficult after all.

By the time I made it back to the ranch, put all my supplies away and tended to the horses and cattle, it was starting to get that perfect time of evening when the shadows start stretching out on the east side of the trees. It feels great to sit in the saddle and take in the scent of mountain pine as it blows down to the ranch while hearing my cattle bellowing. Right now if anyone where to ask me about Bishop or the Lawsons, I guess it would go in one ear and out the other with no stopping in between.

I was almost done carrying water over to Rugers water tank when I noticed a rider coming down the road. Not taking any chances I walked over to the barn door and grabbed my rifle, which was leaning up against it, then slowly moved back a few feet so I couldn't be seen until they were at the barn. When the rider stopped in front of the barn I stepped out with my rifle pointed forward but quickly dropped it down to my side. It was my ole friend Buck. He looked at my rifle then back at me and said, "what the heck Lucas, you expecting trouble"? I felt a little embarrassed then told him, "Sorry Buck, I guess I was just a little on edge tonight, so climb on down and lets talk on the porch".

Buck tied his horse up by the barn and we walked on over to the cabin porch where those old rocking chairs were waiting for us. I told Buck, "Have yourself a seat and I'm gonna fetch us something to drink, and if your hungry there is bowl of nuts on that bench I got from town today". When I came back out and handed Buck his glass he said to me, "Speaking of nuts, have you gone loco, the whole town has been talking about you running those two boys down with your horse, but then to most they were hoping you would finish them off". "Oh, it was nothing", I replied, "they were just causing trouble so I decided to put an end to it by releasing the fear of God into them. He said, "Well it certainly worked cause after you left town I heard those boys saddled up and headed out to there place faster than a couple of scared jack rabbits, and for them to leave the saloon that early, they must have really had the fear put on them".

Buck told me he didn't come out this way just to tell me how crazy I was, but he had heard I might be needing to move my cattle from up near the dugout on down to Ophir. "Dang Buck," I said, "I was only in town for about an hour, how in the world does this get out so fast and especially to you when you live just south of me". He admitted that he was having breakfast over at the café but didn't see or hear anything from there. It was afterward when he went to the hardware store that a group of town folk were standing around along my cousin Gregg that all the information was coming out.

This made no matter anyway so I told him all about Mr. Bishops claim and ownership of the land being an inheritance from his dad. I continued saying, "Now Mr. Bishop asked if I would come on up tomorrow and we would talk about the grazing, so come first light I reckon I will be heading that way with the hopes I can finish out the grazing there and not have to move them till later", so with that in mind I also told Bishop I wouldn't tell anyone his business, so just bear that in mind".

Seeing how this might be more of a touchy business deal Buck didn't come right out and say that he was coming with me, instead he kinda beat around the bush then finally asked me if it would be alright if he went along with me so he could meet the new neighbor. I saw no harm in this, in fact I thought it would be a great idea. But I did feel the need to let him in on what to expect out of the man Jefferson Bishop. I explained to him, " Now Buck, this man is as hard as a rock and takes no guff off anyone, in fact he took those two boys today onto the ground before I could even wink, but I will bet ya that he is a fair man and honest as the day is long". Of course ole Buck has never been afraid of anything or anybody so he simply replied, "Thank ya Lucas, I was sure hoping it would be ok if I went along". Then I also needed to add one more thing in about Mr. Bishop, so I told him, "Now here is the kicker Buck, this man strongly reminds me of myself, and one other person, but when you hear this other persons name you may want to think twice about going with me, and that other person is you". "Holy Cow" yelled out Buck, "All that rolled up into one man, why this entire Greenhorn valley aint got a chance, they will be heading down the hill like a forest fire is nipping at their backside".

I think we sat there on the porch the rest of the night cracking jokes about this new adventure and even trying to figure out a common ground in which we could all get along with our new neighbor. With all this talking, joking and even the trouble in town, I honestly believed than one of these days there would be three of us old timers setting on the porch sipping a little whiskey and talking about some newcomers to the area and realizing that we have all been there at one time or another. And that third person setting there with us would be Jefferson Bishop himself. But for now Buck said he needed to get back home and told me that he would see me at first light in the morning.

Even though I had been up long before first light, as to be expected here comes Buck riding up to the cabin. I had already been waiting on the porch with my horse hitched to the post and ready to go, so I just went from the rocking chair to the saddle. Buck asked me if I had any thoughts on making a deal over grazing. "No I haven't", I said "In fact there isn't a whole lot of things to make a deal with, he is a prospector and I am cowboy, there is just not too many things in common there". It didn't take long to get to Mr. Bishops place so before we went on down we stayed on the hillside for a little bit longer watching my cattle graze just north of the dugout and trying to see if we could see Mr. Bishop out and around. We saw his mule and a little smoke coming off a campfire, but didn't see Jefferson. I told Buck, "We better get down there and make sure everything is ok".

Buck rode down from one side and I went in from the other but still no Jefferson to be seen. No sooner than we were fixin to ride up to the mine shaft a shot rang out. We made a hard ride over to the dugout for cover, jumped off our horses, and waited to see where the shots were coming from. One more fired off and I saw the gun smoke coming from the mine. So I told Buck, "You wait here, I'll bet that's Bishop, but he was expecting only me and not two riders". I started walking up the hill yelling out his name and telling him who I was, but at the same time making sure I had some quick cover in site. Sure enough here comes Jefferson walking out of the mine entrance with a rifle in hand. As he got a little closer he yelled out, "I could have picked both of you off if I wanted to, and besides I wasn't looking for two riders this morning only one". I explained to him that Buck was a friend and neighbor that I had ask to come with me, not only to meet him but he also helps bring the cattle down every year. Once Jefferson accepted my story and started to calm down, I motioned for Buck to come on up.

I introduced Mr. Bishop to Buck and told him we have lived here the better part of our lives and know the country inside out. So if he needed help to just look us up cause we would be around somewhere. Jefferson then said to us in his usual manner, "I thank you boys for that, but enough chit chat, we got some business to talk over and its starting to get late in the day". I glanced over to Buck with a half smirk knowing I didn't have to say anything cause the morning sun just rose above the trees a few moments ago. I replied to him, "Your sure right Mr. Bishop, lets get down to it and see what we can figure out, and if you don't mind would please lower that rifle a little bit". He looked at his rifle then up at the two of us and said, "Oh heck, I think I can trust the both ya, but stop calling me Mr., either call me Jefferson or Bishop cause my folks never gave me the name Mr." "Alright", I said, " We'll just call you Jefferson, which makes me Lucas and this is Buck, now I've got a few ideas but would sure like to hear what you might have in mind first".

We walked on down to his campfire where he had some logs laying for something to set on and even a pot of coffee hanging over the hot coals. Jefferson started out by telling us he looked the mine over pretty good but it needed more shoring to re-place the bad ones and more for new digging. He then pointed out to me that the trees on his land was few and far between and that some good cedar would sure be nice for all the work he needs to do. He said, "Lucas I saw an area down to the south a ways where hundreds of cedar were". I knew what he was getting at so I told him, " Jefferson, thats part of my ranch down there, in fact I have been cutting cedar out of there for a long time now and have been stock piling them for fence post or anything else". He asked me if part of the deal would be him cutting some of those for his mine and even to help build onto his little dugout cabin. I told him I would just bring him a wagon full tomorrow so he could get started right away.

He told me he didn't want to take any from my pile and didn't mind cutting his own. "Jefferson", I said, "Those piles have been getting mighty big so there is more than enough for your jobs and mine both". With the deal on the cedar I could tell that Jefferson was happy with it and so was I, after all those ole post were going to help us both out quite a bit. But then looking around at his campsite I sure didn't see much when it came to building something, mainly prospector tools, his mule and an old two wheel cart his mule would pull. So without prying into his business I simply asked, "One other thing Jefferson, you said something about building more onto your cabin so if you need some extra tools or even someone to help I'd sure be happy to do so and Buck may even have some free time every now and then". "No Sir", he said, "This ole dugout and that mine is all I have and I don't want anyone else messing around with them", now we can have our business deal but anything after that I will take care of myself".

I kinda figured right about now would be a good time for Buck and I to leave Jefferson to the rest of his day, so as we all stood up from those hard logs I shook his hand and told him, "I sure admire your principles but remember the offer is always there, and I will have a wagon load of cedar up here for you tomorrow". We both bid him a good day then rode off back to the ranch. We stopped again further on up the ridge and looked back towards Jeffersons camp. Buck shaking his head back and forth said to me, "I'm sure glad your property joins him and not mine, that ole boy is one of a kind". "You sure aint wrong there Buck", I said, "but look at that ole fellow down there almost running from one place to the next, I believe if there is gold in that mine he will find it, and if he wanted to take that ole dugout and build a castle to the sky he would do it, so what ya say Buck, you want to help me load up some post today so I can take it up here tomorrow". He said, "lets get after it, its gonna be dark in another ten hours you know".

The next morning I brought my two draft horses out the corral and hooked them up to the wagon which was already piled high with cedar post. It didn't take us long to have it loaded yesterday, in fact I had almost a full day left over by the time we brought it back down to the barn and put the horses away. I climbed on up, snapped the reigns and off I went to Jefferson Bishops place. I had several questions bugging me about that old mine and one in particular was why his father abandoned it in the first place. Now several years later here comes Jefferson to take claim again. I know there's a heck of a story in there somewhere, but I sure aint gonna ask him.

When I arrived at his homestead I stopped the wagon near a tree grove and went looking for Jefferson so I'll know where to unload the post. I hollered out ever so often as I was walking closer to his dugout but there was no response. So I headed up to the mine still yelling out for him but no Jefferson in site. I stood about fifty feet in front of the mine shaft calling out his name and trying to see inside, when all the sudden I heard a voice ring out "Yee Haw". And like a bat flying out of a cave here comes Jefferson running straight at me then yelled out again, "Fire in hole". Well I sure wasn't born yesterday, I knew exactly what that meant. As soon as I heard that I turned around running just as fast as he was then we both took a nose dive behind some rocks. It was none to soon cause that instant a huge blast came from the mine with a heavy cloud of dust and rocks shooting out of there like a shotgun. Once the rocks stopped flying and the dust died down we came out from behind the rocks and Jefferson looked calmly over at me and said, "Good morning Lucas, what are you doing here". I know I had a dumb founded look on my face when I replied, "I brought the post we talked about, and if you don't mind me asking, what the heck did you just do"? "What does it look like, I sealed the opening, not that its any of your business, now lets go unload your wagon".

I told him the wagon was down by the trees on

the other side of the dugout. He said "Well how did you know, cause that's exactly where I wanted them". Then as we walked closer the horses and wagon weren't there any longer, they were further down the tree line, the wagon was empty, and the sides were busted off. But I'll be dog gone, every single post was laying in the area where he said was a good spot for them. Jefferson looking puzzled said, "Lucas why did you unload the wagon by yourself, I was here to help, but seeing how you did, you could have staked them a little better". Trying to keep calm I quickly replied, "I didn't unload the wagon, your dynamite spooked my horses causing the sides to break, and they took off over yonder", that's why they are all laying here in a scattered mess". Jefferson told me, "Lets just get these post stacked up against the trees like their supposed to be and quit blaming it on your horses". I stood there for longest time looking at the post, then over to Jefferson, then over to my horses and wagon wondering if there was something I missed in this conversation or was I just getting sun stroked on this cool and cloudy day.

I finally stopped the useless wondering and picked up my speed carrying posts and stacking them right where Jefferson wanted them. When every single post was stacked in their rightful place and we both stood stretching looking at our accomplishment, I asked Jefferson, "Would you mind telling me why you sealed the mine shaft, I thought you wanted to dig the mine and that's why you made the claim". Jefferson walked a little closer to me with that hard stern look in his eyes and I didn't know whether to listen or knock him down, but I figured listening was in order. He then said to me, "Lucas, you have been nothing but accommodating ever since I first met you and your still the same, I honestly believe you are a man to be trusted, which is something I haven't come across most of my life, so I feel I can tell you why, so have a seat on those logs and I'll explain".

I couldn't have been more curious about something when he said to have a seat and lets talk, not even the slightest idea, so I sat there with all my attention aimed directly towards him and what he had to say. Jefferson tried sitting but he was just to fidgety so standing and pacing seemed to help him talk a little better. "Lucas" he said, "It was only a few years back when I was given a letter that my Dad had written to me about this place along with some legal documents giving me ownership". He continued saying, " I took my time not doing anything about it because I thought it was just another one of his dreams of chasing something that wasn't there, that is until I started thinking about where he wrote the words, "Seal The Day To The West Then Open A New Day To The East". At this point Jefferson was beginning to look as if he had just seen the hand of God reaching down to him.

Jefferson became more serious while pointing towards the mine shaft which he had just sealed and said, "Lucas, my father was never a man to come right out and give a straight answer to anyone about anything, so I believe that he was trying to tell the story about this mine in his own but confusing way". Now Jefferson was hitting on the right word and that was "confusing", so just as straight faced as him I said, "Jefferson, you are going to have to be a little more simple for this ole cowboy cause I don't know your father at all and I have only known you for about a week, so please get to the point". Jefferson knew he needed to start making sense of this so he finally said, "Ok, I think by sealing the opening of the mine which faces west, a new opening to the east will appear, and that's where the gold should be". With him telling me this I knew he was serious as could be and that I could not say a word to anyone about his idea. So I told him, " If this is true, then you have my word it will not go any further, but don't you think we should go up there and see if there is another opening on the east side".

Jefferson sat there looking at me for a while and then looking up towards the mine for a bit like he was trying to make the biggest decision of his life. I just couldn't take the suspense any longer so I said,

"Ok Jefferson, its like you have told me several times on just about everything, "I don't have all day", so are we going to search for the other opening or not". He looked at me with that one eyebrow arched way up and replied, "Guess there is no need to hesitate now, cause I let you in on this much of my business which means I trust you, so lets go see if we can find it". We took off walking up the hill towards the mine with both of us looking around the area making sure no one was in sight. All it takes is something like this for a man to become suspicious of everything around him and that something is the possibility of finding gold.

We climbed up the rocks above the old mine shaft making our way to the other side of the ridge. Jefferson took off one way and me the other, both of us turning over any loose rocks and tossing limbs laying around. It seemed like for an hour we were crawling around throwing rocks from one side to the other till finally Jefferson yelled out to me, "Over here Lucas, over here quick". I was just as excited as him when he showed me a large rock shooting dust out from around the edges like air was coming out from around it. We both grabbed hold of that rock and pulled and pushed with all our might till it finally it gave way and we both ended up falling backwards. We knew there had to be some hollow ground under that rock or it wouldn't be blowing dust from around it. Then with all our might we gave a last huge tug and the rock went rolling down the hill like a runaway train. I guess our attention was drawn more at the rock hoping it wasn't going to hit anything. Then we quickly looked back at where the rock came from and by golly there was a hole big enough for a bobcat to crawl in and out of but for a man it was just way the heck to small.

I told Jefferson, "well it looks like you found your other entry but I got a feeling you got some hard working days ahead". With his head half way into that hole I'm surprised he even heard me but he turned and looked up at me with one of those intense looks and said, "that's right Lucas, and I will tell you what else is right, that your not to say a word to anyone, not even your horse, cause someone just might hear it". I grabbed his hand pulling him up from the ground but still held on with a firm grip and a stern handshake saying, "Jefferson Bishop, you told me earlier that you could trust me, and now I give you my word that this is only between you and I and the almighty, and he is the one you best be relying on rather than me. He replied, " I suppose your right , so that's all I needed to hear Lucas".

It looked like there might be only a few hours of daylight left so I told Jefferson I needed to get back to the ranch cause my chores have to get done regardless of gold or not, but I would be back up again to check on my cattle soon enough. Which made me think of something else before I left so I asked him, "now Jefferson, with this new hole needing to be a secret, just how are you going to keep it from anyone passing by or even when some hands that come with me to help round up the cattle". " Don't fret on that Lucas", he said, "you may know where its at yourself, but you will never see it, so to anyone else it just doesn't even exist". I figured it will be hidden somehow but didn't need to know how so I bid him a good evening and walked back down to my wagon. I gave the reigns to my team a snap and headed back up the hill towards the ranch, but like I usually do I stopped on the ridge to look back towards Bishops place. This time I could see Jefferson still standing near the spot where we found the new shaft, except looking my way as if thinking he wasn't doing anything until I was out of sight. I guess I know when my presence aint appreciated so with another good snap of the reigns we headed back to the ranch.

The entire time it took me getting back to the ranch house I couldn't get my thoughts away from Jefferson as to will he be ok or what if some ruthless sidewinders happened upon his home will he be able to handle them. From what I know and have seen out of Jefferson Bishop I think it might be the sidewinders that should be worried. Then for some odd reason as I was driving my team down into the barn yard I thought of some words which my cousin, Tall Bull, told me one time, he said, "seek out your enemy, then your friends will follow". These words I felt had something to do with me, Bishop, and any dealings we had together other wise I don't think it would have been on my mind.

So for the rest of the evening I was busy taking care of my wagon team, checking on the horses and cattle that were gathering around the barn. Then I finished up by checking the water tank under the upper windmill. When I started back to the cabin I saw three riders coming down the road towards the house. I gave my horse an extra kick and made it back to the cabin before they rode in. I wasn't taking any chances so I grabbed my rifle and sat there tall in the saddle waiting for them to come on down. I don't know what had gotten into me, but just as these strangers rode on in I cocked the lever on my rifle, pointed it towards them, then yelled out, "state your business boys". I believe this welcome wasn't what they were expecting nor is it what I would normally do. But even still they all held their hands straight up into the air. Seeing this I began to loosen my trigger grip, but just a little. The one I would call the spokesman of the group introduced himself as Wilbur Smith and other two were his sons, William and Terrance. I told them, "As I said before gents, state your business". The old man said, "We're not looking for any trouble, I just need to find my cousin, his name is Jefferson Bishop, have you heard of him". I'm thinking that things may just get a little more complicated around here for a while.

I sat there quiet for a few seconds with my rifle still pointing their direction. I knew I had to say something but I didn't want that something to be an all out lie either. Just so my thoughts could buy a little more time I told him, "well now Mr. Smith you say his name is Jefferson Bishop, can you describe him at all, and by the way, you can put your hands down but keep them laying right there on your saddle horn". The dad started in trying to describe Jefferson which was all pretty general and could have fit most anyone, until he hit on one thing, and that was a slight limp favoring his left side. Still not wanting to say I knew Jefferson and where he's at I told him, "you know there has been several strangers pass through this area and they usually end up going to town for one thing or another, so maybe that's your best bet, go in there and ask around". The two boys were getting real fidgety in there saddle and one them loudly said, "Pa, this ole man aint gonna tell us anything". I raised my rifle on up to shoulder height then the Dad turned to his sons and said in a scolding voice, "you boys shut up and mind your manners". He then turned back towards me and said, "Sorry for that, we do appreciate your advice Mr. so we best be going". They all three turned their horses around and quickly rode down the rode, and I could hear the dad hollering and cussing at the two boys the whole time.

I watched them till they were out of sight and on the road to town, then I rode on west towards the tree line so I could take the back trail over to Jeffersons place. Its gonna be dark before I get there but my horse and myself know the country so well we can ride it blindfolded. I thought this would be best in case those fellows waited up ahead somewhere to see if I was going anywhere, perhaps to warn Bishop, of course I am, but just being careful about it. I rode in from the west and could see a campfire and a lantern up by the mine so I stopped a ways back from his place and called out for Jefferson.

My first thought was those Smiths following me, that is until a heard a voice say, "I will shoot you off your horse right now unless you start talking". That voice was Jefferson for sure, so I started talking just like he asked. Then he went on telling me about how many times so far I could have been shot coming up here and especially this time of night. I swear this man must have hearing and a nose like a dog. I started telling him about the three men who rode into the ranch asking about him and that they claimed they were cousins. Jefferson said he didn't have any family left after his dad died several years ago but asked if they gave their names. I said, "Yes they did, the older one said he was Wilbur Smith and the other two were his sons, William and Terrance, so Jefferson I came up here this late at night cause I thought you should be warned of their arrival before tomorrow, I steered them towards town, but they just might find out your where abouts".

Jefferson started telling me, "Yeah, their relation alright but very distant, and if there is ever a family of black sheep, it would certainly be them, so I thank you Lucas for letting me know but if they come around here I know exactly how to handle them". I offered a second gun for him but he didn't want any part of that offer and still claimed he will handle it himself. I saw no need to argue with him on his claim because I have seen him handle himself pretty good like with the Lawson brothers in town. But on the other hand I do have cattle up around here that need to be checked on every now and then and perhaps even checked on more often then usual cause there has been some hungry mountain lions around here lately. So I told Jefferson, "What ever you say Jefferson, I'll be going back now so just keep your eyes peeled come daylight". I did hear Jefferson come up with a thank you as I rode off into the night heading back to the ranch.

After a restless nights sleep because of all that

went on yesterday and then being out on the trail so dog gone late, I finally crawled out of bed, put some coffee on and went outside for fresh air. Even this early I kept my eyes and ears peeled thinking someone would be riding in or even hearing gun-shots echo around the hills coming from Bishops place. The sun was already up and nothing like that has happened yet so I just hoped for the best and maybe things will stay that way. I was always one that got by pretty good on wishful thinking, that is until I got to thinking too much. I for sure never have any problems keeping busy and today riding over to Bucks place has been on my mind, not for any special reason other than to check on him and see if come next month he will still be able to help bring cattle back down to the lower pasture. Of course the name Jefferson Bishop will certainly come up, but I did give my word to Jefferson that I would not talk about his business to anyone, and I meant it.

Later after coffee I saddled up and took a short cut through the woods to Bucks place cause I also wanted to check on the water level coming down the Greenhorn creek cause it has been dry so far and all the snow melt has come and gone for some time now. The creek comes within about two hun-dred yards of Bucks house so when I got there and dismounted just to run my hands through the water and let Ruger have a drink, I could hear some voices coming from Bucks cabin so I figured it was only him and his sons out there working on something. I decided to just take the reigns and walk on in but the closer I got those voices sounded as if someone was arguing. When I got a little closer and could see through the trees I saw Buck standing out front of his cabin along with three riders. Taking a better look I could see it was those dad burn cousins of Bishops, I mounted back up and Ruger and I come running out of those woods towards the house like a scared deer in lion country. Buck turned around with eyes as big as silver dollars and the Smiths were trying to control their spooked horses.

Buck backed up several feet and I brought my horse in between him and the Smiths then Buck loudly said, "good morning Lucas", then he looked at the Smiths and said, "this is my friend and neighbor Lucas Clay". "We've met", said Wilbur Smith, "and do you always come charging in just to visit a neighbor". I sternly replied back, "only when I hear voices being raised and I have a friend in the middle of it, so Buck is there a problem here this morning". Buck came back at me with, "Well Lucas there wasn't any problem on my part, but I cant rightly say the same for these fellows, and now that you're here I'll bet their problem doesn't seem that important anymore". Then to be expected out any brat the sassy one of the Smith boys said to his dad, "Pa, I aint gonna take this from these ole men, they just don't want to tell us anything about uncle Jefferson and that aint right". I turned my horse towards that kid, gave him a good spurring and running right into him. His horse jumped up throwing that boy onto the ground. Then within an instant I pulled my side arm out and pointed it straight at the old man. I stared into his eyes and said, "Mr. Smith, in this valley we welcome most anyone, and the ones we don't, then heaven help you, so which is it going to be, a welcomed stranger or just another tombstone, which is it, cause Buck and I have things to do today".

Mr. Smith acted as if he wanted to say something against our grain until he looked over towards Buck and saw that he had a double barrel shotgun pointed right at his two sons. That even surprised me, cause where in the heck was he hiding that scatter gun all this time. But then I should have known cause when it comes to Buck you always approach with caution. Just by looking at their faces I had a feeling they were thinking that now is not the time to be saying the wrong thing or making any move that could be the wrong one. In other words, cooperation seemed to be in order on their part. So I waited patiently for his answer.

Well Mr. Clay" the dad said, "It sure looks like we got off on the wrong foot, and as I told you yesterday we are not looking for any trouble, so we will just ride on out here and leave you two alone". I went ahead and holstered my side arm but I am sure Buck still had his scatter gun up and ready. So without saying a word we watched them ride on out till they were out of range. I then turned to Buck and asked him," what was all the arguing about I overheard". He started telling me he had just sent his sons on up the hill to fix some fences when these men rode into his ranch and started asking about that prospecting fellow Jefferson Bishop. He said he didn't get a good feeling about them so he just acted like he never heard of him hoping they would say why they wanted to find him. Buck then told me they started yelling about all the stupid people around here not knowing anything and that's when he started backing up towards the hitching post yelling back at them. Buck said, "Lucas my shotgun was leaning up against the post and I almost had my hands on it but that's when you come riding in like a war party of one man, but I'm glad you did, so thank you".

Buck asked me what brought me over here and that he was glad I showed up when I did. I told him , "well I thought I came over to see if you are still going to help next month bringing the cattle down to the lower pastures, but I was also going to tell you those men were at my place yesterday and was asking the same thing, and told me that Bishop was his cousin, but it kinda looks like you already got your introduction with them". Buck told me they hadn't said anything to him about being any kind of kin, they only said his name and asked if he knew him or even heard about him. I told him," they probably didn't get the chance once I came riding in, and besides after they left my place I took the back way up to Jefferson's to warn him and it turns out they are related, and I gather there is no love lost between them". I told Buck I would get back with him in a couple of days then rode back home.

I didn't want to keep my mind occupied on just this Bishop thing cause I knew that Jefferson could handle about anything that came his way and as far as Buck goes, well lets just say that if I hadn't of rode in when I did there would be a whole family of Smiths to load into a wagon and take to the Doc in town for buckshot extraction. So right now I am thinking the best thing for me to do is head back to the ranch and get started on some things that have been put off for too long, darn if I can remember what they are but I'll bet by the time I get there I can think of at least one of them.

For the next several days it seemed like I was thinking of one repair right after another. The cabin, barn, corrals, and even the fences that extended on up to the higher pastures. The days just started flowing into one another to where it seemed only a couple of days had gone by, but that wasn't the case, these chores had kept me busy for almost a week. So one morning while sitting on the porch with my morning coffee and wondering what to do next, I figured I would ride into town for a few things and maybe even go over to Miss Vicky's café for a darn good breakfast. Needless to say it didn't take me long to convince myself to do just that. I was up and headed to the corral to saddle up my horse and go to town. When I got to town the very first place I went was Miss Vicky's for some flapjacks and ham. Of course the meal played only second to Miss Vicky's smile while she was serving it to you.

My next stop was the hardware store where I needed more nails and some mending wire. As I entered the store Jake Reed the owner called out to me, "Hello there Lucas, what can I do for you today". I told him the few things I needed and he happen to say just for the sake of conversation, "You know Lucas, speaking of nails, that neighbor of yours was in here the other day and bought a bunch of nails along with chicken wire, said he was repairing his house, that's odd aint it Lucas, to repair your house with chicken wire".

Seeing how Jake seemed to think it was a little strange for a prospector to be buying nails and chicken wire I asked him, "Do you know much about mining Jake"? He told me he didn't know too much about it other than some of the mining tools he sells. So I explained to him how to use the nails and chicken wire in the mine and the dugout cabin. He then said, "Well regardless of what he is going to use them for, he sure turned out to be a popular fellow cause that same day some men came in here asking if I knew or heard of him". "Well what did you tell them"? I asked him. He continued saying, "About all I could tell them was that I know of him, but before I could say anything else the two Lawson brothers were standing over there looking at some new pistols I just got in when one of them walked over and told this stranger that they knew him and that they were friends, and I knew that wasn't true because I saw the fight you and Bishop had with those two boys out in the street, so the next thing I knew all five of them left the store and headed straight over to the saloon".

My mind started thinking the worse cause this did happen several days ago and now we're talking five idiots not just two and if all of them were to visit Jefferson it isn't because they want to have tea. So I gathered up my things and thanked Jake for the supplies and conversation. I headed on out of town thinking once I should get back to the ranch cause it just might be a good idea to take a ride up to Jefferson Bishops place whether I need to check on cattle or not, cause right now I believe I should be checking on him. I have been trying to reason out my bad thoughts but it doesn't seem to be working. Either I am going to find a massacre with everyone on the ground or a nice reunion with laughter and a good game of cards going on, or perhaps Bishop actually working on his cabin. So back at the barn I put my stuff away, got back in the saddle and took off for Bishops place at a full run.

Once I topped the ridge where I could see Bishops place, visions of a war zone were popping into my mind, I paused for only a minute to look around and saw no such scene, instead I could see Jeffersons mule in a corral down by the trees but no other horses and no people at all. Taking this as a good sign I gave Ruger a swift kick and down to his camp I rode with more dust behind me than a stampede. I didn't bother dismounting because I wasn't trying to be quiet, it was a lot quicker to ride from one spot to the next, starting with his dugout then on up to the mine. Without seeing any sign of Jefferson or anyone else I then remembered the new opening over the top of the rocks. I rode around the rocks till I came upon the spot which Jefferson and I had dug out a huge boulder that was hiding the mines back opening. I brought Ruger to a dead stop and we stood there in amazement along with gasp of relief. There was Jefferson Bishop with his arms full of timber walking over to the mine shaft whistling like he never saw me riding up.

I dismounted and tied my horse to the nearest brush then went over to Jefferson, who then acted a little surprised that I was there. Without bringing too much alarm to him about the things I heard in town and that was why I was there, I told him that I was in the area and thought I would make a friendly visit. Jefferson laid down the timber he was holding and looked at me with that stern stare when one eyebrow shoots up on his forehead and said, "That's bull Lucas, you came up here cause you heard there might be something wrong, like those cousins of mine or even those two dim wit brothers from town, but as you can see I am just fine". "Well dog gone it Jefferson", I replied, "Your right, I did hear something in town about all five of them talking about you, but I never heard what they were talking about, so I just assumed it was not good". Jefferson told me to have a seat on that rock beside me and he would tell me all about what happened around here the last couple of days.

In Jefferson's usual way, letting me know that he has always been capable of handling anything or anyone that came around, I sat there listening to what he had to say. And so he confirmed exactly what first came to my mind when those cousins came looking around for him. He told me the Smith family, meaning William, Terrance, and their dad Wilbur rode into his camp just the other day morning acting as if they had been looking for him for such a long time because they missed the old days of being a close family. Jefferson then stood up, walked a few feet over and spit some tobacco juice smack dab on the head of a rattle snake that was stretched out beside a bush next to us. I must have been listening to him so intensely I didn't even notice a snake nearby. Anyway that snake picked up some speed and crawled as fast as possible away from us. Jefferson sat back down and said, " Lucas, that's one way to get rid of a snake that's coming your way, show them what your made of and don't back down".

I sat there watching the snake slither away with Jefferson's tobacco juice burning on his head. I don't believe he had to go into much detail as to how he took care of his cousins, because by now I have known Jefferson enough that I can figure out his explanations to his actions. But one thing kept bugging me so I asked, "Jefferson, I get your point, but what makes you think they wont come back"? Jefferson told me had a feeling something like this would happen, whether it was his no good cousins who were always after quick money and no work or even some local people like the Lawson brothers. "So Lucas", he continued saying, "The day I blew the opening to the mine is the day the answer to your questions and everyone else was answered, if the mine is blown, then it is no longer a mine". I then asked him about the supplies he bought in town and he replied, "You watch my dugout house grow Lucas, that's where my supplies are going, and no one needs to know any different".

Throughout Bishops talk about the last few days I also was aware of the fact that he never once said anything about his new mine shaft, whether he had been working on it or even found anything. I think its an unwritten code that asking a prospector if he found anything is like asking a gambler what kind of cards is he holding before the game is done, you just don't do it unless you really like the taste of lead. I was still curious about his kin folk so I asked him, "Jefferson I'm pretty sure you didn't spit on your cousins head which made them turn and run away, so how in the world did their visit end"? He told me that once they started asking about any gold in the mine he took them up to the shaft and told them to look for themselves. They all three climbed off their horses and almost ran over to where the opening used to be and once they saw nothing but rocks piled up and some old timbers laying around then Wilbur turned and asked him if I had blown the shaft myself. "Lucas", he said, "you may not know this, but once a miner blows a shaft that means the hole is worked out, nothing is left and never will be, and those Smiths know that as a fact, so when they finally finished their moaning, cussing and accusing me of drawing the last nugget out of there, then they got back on the saddles and headed north". Being a little surprised I told Jefferson that sounded awful easy, so he did confess a little more and said, "Well maybe not that easy, I think when I shot Wilbur's hat of his head then picked up some rocks and threw them at the two boys horses that made them hurry along a little faster". I tried my best not to laugh but by golly that's the Jefferson Bishop I know, very un-predictable and ready to strike at anytime , in fact as he just proved to me earlier even a rattle snake aint got anything over him. Still keeping my expres-sion down to half grin I told Jefferson, "Well it looks like once again there wasn't anything to worry about here cause I don't think even a rabid coyote would dare to cross your place without an invite, so I reck-on I'll let you get back to working on your chores around here and I'll head back home.

The only thing I didn't ask Jefferson after he told me about his company was if the Lawson brothers were anywhere around his place. After all the last I heard was that all five of those scoundrels were at the saloon together and I assume talking about Jefferson. I am sure if they had shown up then he would have told me about it. I'm also pretty sure the Smiths will never be back and as far as the other two, well I believe they can be handled very easy also.

When it comes to Jefferson Bishop, his new place and the secrets that seem to be surrounding it I figure the best thing for me to do is simply watch, listen and don't ask questions and don't give opinions. There is only one place and set of good listening ears that I have ever been able to speak my peace while reasoning things out, and that's right here in the saddle. For a long time ole Ruger has been listening to me go on about one thing or another, and not once has he ever ignored me or told me to be quiet. So for now the best thing for us both is getting back to the ranch for some supper and a little rest.

As I was riding closer to the fork in the road where one way goes down to my ranch and the other to town I was seeing two riders also nearing the fork. The little rest I was thinking of may just have to wait a little longer cause I was starting to recognize the riders as the Lawson brothers. I pulled the rifle from my saddle sheath and laid it across my legs while still riding closer to them. Once we were about fifty feet away from each other I stopped and so did they. I spoke up first and asked, "What you boys doing today, just out for a ride or looking for trouble"? Clem answered back, "No sir Mr. Clay we aint looking for any trouble, least ways not with you or Mr. Bishop either, we're looking for three men by the name of

Smith, a father and two sons, have you seen them". "Why you looking", I asked, Cause from what I hear the five of you went to the saloon the other night like a bunch of trouble making old friends, but I guess you aint friends anymore".

Right about this time I could see they wanted to get a little mouthy because of my question, that is until I re-positioned the rifle on my lap. It was almost like trying to say something with your mouth full of steak, the wanted to say something then figured swallowing their words was the best thing to do. So I told the both of them, "You boys listen real good to me, I don't know your business with them and I don't want to know, but if either one of you expect to live as long as me then you best turn your horses around and go back home, grow a garden, paint your house, or get a job, I don't much care, but if you still want to be the idiots you are, then take the road to Denver, cause that's where the Smiths were going". They acted as if I didn't know what I was talking about, but still curious enough to ask me how I would know that. Of course anytime I can put the fear of God into these two boys I'll take the time hoping that one day they just might see the light.

I raised my rifle up off of my legs and secured it back into my saddle sheath. This might have made them twitch a little bit when I raised it up, but then that was my intention. I walked my horse closer to them making it mighty uncomfortable for them, then said, "I was told this by their cousin, Mr. Bishop, who made them wish they had never come to this country, so if you still want to go find them, that's ok, I'll just get a hold of the sheriff next week and tell him the situation as to why your home has been abandoned, then he will have to start some sort of public auction to get rid of your house and all your things including those horses". Well instantly young Albert spoke out, "What are you talking about Lucas, our mama gave us that place its our home"! "That it is Albert", I replied, "but you boys wont be coming back if you head to Denver looking for the Smiths, and its just not right to let all your good stuff and that house just whither away when some other folks could make some good use of it". I then rode my horse between them and said, "Think about it boys, right now I have work to do", then I rode off while they still sat there arguing back and forth.

I probably wont know for several days if those two went to Denver or got scared off and decided to go back home. With as much trouble as those two have been it may concern me for about thirty seconds and then I'll be over it. By the end of the week I will have to take the wagon into town and load up feed supplies for the horses and for the cabin, so I reckon either I will see those two in town or hear something about them being gone. I know it's a hard choice if I had to pick between the two, but I am kinda hoping they didn't go to Denver.

So many things have been going on this past several weeks, things that have not been my usual routine. Ever since the arrival of Jefferson Bishop I have been up and down that north mountain trail a dozen times, checking on cattle as my main reason, but actually checking on the new neighbor because of all the uncertainty and mystery he brought with him. I will never try to find fault in people no matter if they are strangers or someone I know. I figure any faults will come out sooner or later and I'll catch onto it in a wink and deal with it at that time. And believe me, there is a lot of folks out there that let you know right off the bat exactly what their faults are. And just maybe that's the best way, cause then you can deal with it just as fast and never have to mess with it again.

So far I have not found that fault in Jefferson Bishop, the kind of fault that makes you want to shake some sense into someone or simply turn away and try not to cross their path again. He can be pretty aggravating and hard headed a lot, but the admiration and respect for values and survival, well, out weighs the other. So I guess that's why I have taken all the time from my normal daily life making sure in my own mind that he is safe and doing well by using the cattle as an excuse to go check on him. But now

I am completely convinced that Jefferson will come out the victor when confronted with trouble like I have seen lately. I looked down at my horse and said, Thanks for listening Ruger, now lets get home.

This past couple of months have been some of the most unpredictable and busiest I have seen around here in a long time. Trying to get every fence mended whether its replacing post or stringing out and stretching more wire. In just a few short days its going to be time to gather the cattle I have grazing on higher ground and get them back down before winter comes on. Buck and his boys have been a big help when it comes to riding fences that connect his ranch with mine but I don't have that option on the west and north sides because it connects to the mountain range and its tough enough riding it, let alone putting fence on it, besides with all the elk, deer and a few buffalo over there a fence wouldn't last long.

I haven't given up on ole Bishop, in fact a few days ago while in town I was hearing a few comments, but the most news came from Jake Reed the owner of the hardware store. It seems Jefferson had been in there at least once a week getting more chicken wire and long spikes, except this time he had ordered several bags of lime. More than likely to coat the walls of his house to keep the bugs and water out. I really shouldn't have asked this of Mr.

Reed but I did anyway, "Now Jake you don't have to say anything if don't want, but does Mr. Bishop have a charge account with you"? Jake leaned over the counter a little closer to me and said, "Lucas you know I would never gossip about any of my customers, but you and I go back a long ways and I know you can keep quiet about this, but every time Jefferson Bishop places an order or just buys what I have on hand, he always pays in cash, in fact he will always say to me, our business is our business". Knowing Jefferson the way I do, I knew this was just another way of survival for him. I told Mr. Reed, "You did good Jake, and for sure I will keep quiet". All of this would seem so common in any other case, but in this one we have a lone prospector claiming a mine from his father and all he has is a mule, a cart and some camping supplies. I sure didn't see any gold boxes laying around anywhere.

I knew that no one else around here were putting two and two together like I have, but then they haven't been helping Jefferson they way I have either. The very worst thought I could have would be that he has been a bank robber or any other kind of outlaw. In fact I believe I would knock the tar out of anyone who suggested that. So before my mind starts wandering off to things I know nothing about I'll just go up to Jeffersons place tomorrow which is the day before roundup and see what I can see. I have always been a good judge of character when knowing lies from the truth and its never failed me yet. But then there was that time when my sister Carla told me she was an expert shot right after placing an apple on my head. She got the apple alright, and besides, my hat covers that little scalped part anyway.

Next morning I saddled up and took off towards the upper trail leading to Bishops place instead of the road. I guess there might be a few more doubts left in me, but I knew they would all go away shortly. As I came out of the wooded trail where I could see Jeffersons place along with some of my cattle near the plateau I paused for the longest time perhaps waiting for my thoughts to clear before going on down or simply looking around at the progress Jefferson had made. Whatever the case may be, I was just too far away to see much and didn't want to be caught spying on him. So I rode on down to his cabin and as it came closer I didn't recognize the place at all. What use to be a small dugout shelter is now a full pueblo type home, perhaps ten times bigger than when I saw it last. A lot of it was still dugout into the hillside but large walls of adobe and even a porch stretched out along the front. Shoot fire, he even built an attached lean to for fire wood.

As I rode up front of the house Jefferson stepped out from the door with a surprised look and said,

"Well he Lucas, what brings you here"? I climbed down from my horse then Jefferson grabbed the reigns and said, "Lets tie your horse up over here by the tree Lucas, it more shady there".

It was almost like he was trying to hide something that was inside the house. But what the heck, sometimes he just acts different than most folks and that's fine. But he really did take my horse to the trees and tied him just like a stable owner then asked me, "Well, what's going on today Lucas"? I told him, "tomorrow is roundup day for the cattle up around here so it seemed like a good idea to look things over before I brought help". He was nodding his head and agreeing with me yet still acting like his thoughts were somewhere else. So to change the conversation I told him I almost didn't recognize his house because of being a lot bigger and now with a porch and windows. And then to push my curiosity a little further I said, "Yep, you have put a lot of work, time and money into this place, and it sure looks good, which reminds me, how is your mine coming along, hope things are looking up for you".

Within a second Jefferson stopped looking around and focused his attention straight at me with that one eyebrow shooting up his forehead then asked, "Why do you want to know about my mine, have people been talking about it in town or what". Then he paused for a minute with his head down and his hand raised and said, " I'm sorry for getting snippy Lucas, I guess over the months when folks ask me how my mine is doing its usually been because they want some of what I got, but I don't believe that is your intention, you have proven to be a true friend and one I can trust". Still taken off guard and trying to come back with some sort of a thank you, Jefferson said, "you don't have to say a word Lucas, in fact I would like to give you a little tour of the place starting with the mine shaft you helped me uncover, then down to the house". I figured now is not time to act like I wasn't curious, cause I was, so with saying very little I let Jefferson lead the way up the rocky hill to the other side where the new opening was. Then what I saw would be the envy of any miner who wants to keep things under hat.

Jefferson had taken several of those cedar timbers I had brought to him and created one heck of a boom over the entry along with pulleys. Now the best part about it was that he had to show me where it all was when we got up there. He took several branches, tumble weeds and what ever it took to make it look like all the rest of the trees and brush scattered around. He pulled a couple large branches back out of the way and there stood the frame with the pulley with heavy rope hanging down into the mine shaft. With a big ole grin he looked at me and said, "You see Lucas, you didn't even know where it was till I showed you, and we were standing only a few feet away". I could tell he was anxious to show me this cause he was acting like a kid with a new toy and I was just as surprised to see it.

Jefferson laid the branches back over the boom then told me, "now Lucas I'll bet your also wondering if all of this has been worth it or not, in other words is there any gold in there, well now comes the part of our friendship called trust, so lets go down to the house". I told Jefferson on the way down, "You don't have to be showing me any of this if you don't want to". I just hope he doesn't have to shoot me afterwards.

We walked up to the cabin porch and Jefferson swung that new heavy door open and told me to step on in. The light was shining through the window to where I could see new adobe walls and more rooms with their own doors. But by the way he has been talking I think there is more here than meets the eye.

As I looked around I saw that not only the outside walls were adobe, but the inside walls as well. I wanted to say this would be the reason he was buying all the lime bags from the hardware but If I said anything like that it would look like I was putting my nose where it doesn't belong even though Jake simply offered the information. I turned back around to compliment Jefferson on his place and when I did, he was standing on the other side of the room with a rifle pointed my way. I admit I have been fooled before on things but never lured into a mans home so he could shoot me. My hand instinctively went straight to my holster and Jefferson yelled out, Don't move Lucas". With that I stopped my attempt to draw because I have learned that when a man has the drop on you and starts talking, it always means there is more to say. But by golly what he had to say made me feel pretty foolish.

Jefferson cocked the lever back slowly while telling me, "There is a snake down at your feet so be still". In an instant he pulled the trigger of that rifle and pieces of that floor went flying all over the room. I looked down see if he had killed the snake and I didn't see one anywhere. I was moving around with my own gun drawn at this time looking from side to side and trying to see the floor through all the dust and still no snake. I looked over at Jefferson and said, " Where the heck is the snake"? He stood there with his rifle to his side and a half way grin then told me, "Well, maybe it was just a shadow moving, but it sure looked like a snake from here". I stood there looking at him with one of the most curious looks a man could ever come up with, which was a cross between, what the heck and have you lost your mind. I believe my attitude at this time prompted him to say, "Ok Lucas there was no snake, I did it to convince myself that you know me well enough that

I wouldn't shoot you and that you wouldn't draw on me". This was not making any sense to me at all, in fact I was thinking he has been working in that mine way to long.

When I started going off on Jefferson like a parent scolding his kids for burning the barn down, I believe he started thinking he might have gone about this the wrong way. My hands were already flying all over the place, I could feel my face getting hot and probably red as a beet. He laid his rifle up against the wall and told me, "I reckon you got a right to be mad Lucas, but you will get over it in a minute or two". Still not totally calmed down I turned with both hands pointed down to the floor where he shot and said to him, " look here Jefferson, in order to tell me something you even had to but a big hole in your floor". But as I kept looking down to where I was pointing, I was seeing this bright shine where the bullet had gone through, then my arguing seemed to slow down as I started looking closer to blown away area on the floor till finally I had to kneel down and wiped away the dust around the area where he shot.

I knelt down and even took my shirt sleeve and rubbed the area to get a better look, I looked up at him and said, "Jefferson you have got to be kidding me, this is gold in your floor". And then with a response that once again put me on the edge he grabbed his rifle and shot into the wall just above my head but this time I held it back and didn't do anything more than stand up and wiped away the dust from the new bullet hole he just put into the wall. And there it was, the glimmer of gold shining within the wall of this house and like the streets of heaven it was also below your feet.

I stood there with dust all over me from his target practice looking at the holes he created for me so I could see his secret. Desperately trying to find the words to say to him that would make sense of what I have just seen, I had nothing, and I mean nothing at all other than wiping the dust from my shirt and rubbing my eyes. Still wiping dust from my arms try-ing to see a little better I started walking to the door and told Jefferson, "I need to go outside for a while".

I opened the door I made sure Jefferson walked went ahead of me onto the porch, I grabbed his shoulders which made him swing around to look at me, then within a split second my fist landed on Jefferson's jaw like a hammer on a nail. I swear that old man went flying ten feet off the porch and down onto the dusty ground below. He laid there for al-most a minute then raised up rubbing his face and said, "I believe I deserved that, but I sure didn't think it would be that hard, so can we talk now". I think that's all it took for me start feeling better about this just by working off a little tension. I walked on over to the steps and sat down while Jefferson was shaking his head and still rubbing his jaw, finally managed to get up and sit on the steps also.

We sat there in silence for a little while then he began saying, "Lucas I have spent my entire life working hard for my gains while not trusting anyone in the process, that is until I came here to claim what my father had worked many years ago, within this old mine I found a few of my fathers writings which have given me a new look on life and the people I run into. Lucas, believe me when I say it isn't all about me and it isn't all about the gold, but it is all about how you leave this life and what you leave behind". Right now my full attention was directed on Jefferson's words yet feeling a little guilty about my outburst I let him continue saying. "So let me get to the point Lucas, this mine is full of gold, but as you can see I have hidden the opening while at the same time taking out a fortune and hiding it within the floor and walls of this common adobe home, I have done this to assure it will not be stolen or even taken over by some crooked relation like the Smith family, but at the same time I have put a burden of truth upon you Lucas, and that is only because you are a man to be trusted. And because of that, I also know that when my time comes that same trust will make sure my place will be used for something good and noble".

I have had many friends in my lifetime, some have past on and many still remain, but I cant remember if anyone has ever shown their trust in such away as Jefferson has done. As off the wall as it may seem, his intentions were plain and simple with only one outcome, the truth. I stood up from that porch walking a few feet out before turning around looking at Jefferson Bishop sitting there on the porch of his new treasured house then said, " Jefferson what you have shown and told me here today I will never talk about , but what you have just shared with me as a friend has taken on a whole new meaning, I am sure as well as you, that one of these days that meaning will have to have an outcome". Jefferson looking back at me with one of the most serious looks said, "And that it will Lucas, that It will, and by the way, I will be here tomorrow for roundup and will help take your cattle back down to the valley, and if you have any doubts, that mule out there will let me rope anything I have a need to". I said to Jefferson, "I have no doubts about that at all, in fact if your going to help you will get your chance to do just that".

As I walked on down to the trees where my horse was tied I was feeling as if I just left a combination of a battle field, a session of congress and bible study all rolled into one. As crazy at that may seem there is one thing for sure, I knew I was leaving Bishops place today a better and perhaps wiser man than when I arrived, even though the presentation was off the wall it will never be forgotten and the outcome would be the same. If you cant trust your friends, then you really don't have any friends at all.

WHEN THE NORTH WIND BLOWS

A Winters Wrath

By
Rod Shahan

CHAPTER 5

When the North Wind Blows

A Winters Wrath

SOME FOLKS MAY think its down right silly to hear me talk about how the ranch will hold more information than a dictionary but this place will actually forecast the seasons and sometimes the weather. But I guess rightly so because it is hard to describe to someone the smell of leather from your saddle when it becomes a little more richer before a rain, or when the lord sends out that last burst of heat before fall, the smell isn't that of a hot summer day, it's the sweet smell of the leaves as they are making their final treetop appearance. Yes, this place will let you know every day what is to come, and I will listen ever so closely as I ride through the pastures mending fences and going into the trees looking for any stray or hurt calves. Most of the time I know what month it is, but when it comes to a day, then that's when my memory ends, maybe because its not that important. After all I don't reckon my life is based or judged on schedules of sorts, its how I prepare for the next day and accept the outcome, cause you really don't have a choice.

And now the changing of the season has started. The aspen leaves are turning from their bright green to a speckled yellow, a few more black bears are coming down to fill their bellies before winter and the nights are getting colder. Which means its also time for me to hook the wagon to my draft team and head to the forest to cut up some firewood from all the downed trees. I have some left over from last winter but not near enough to get through this one. There has been a lot of beetle kill on the ponderosa up there, probably more than I can chop for the next several winters.

Just as soon as I tighten some of the fence wire ahead it will be about that time of day to head back to the cabin. With the sun still shining bright as it starts to touch the tree tops I could feel the beginning of the cool breeze as it slowly moves down the mountain side. So I reckon I had better hurry and finish here if I want my horses fed and a warm cabin before nightfall.

I certainly didn't miss getting up early to stoke

the fire in that old pot belly every morning over this past summer. But I am not going to complain about cool mornings either, that is until I wake up and start seeing my breath in front of me. But this morning is calling only for a few more logs to make some coffee and a few warmed over biscuits. So while coffee is cooking I headed on out to hook up my horses to the wagon, gather up my tools and get it all ready to go up for firewood. It seemed to be a pleasant morning with only a cool breeze and a few stretched out group of clouds across the moonlit sky. One of the many things my Cherokee upbringing taught me was reading the night sky. How they change their places with the moon and then how the moon changes it position as the morning sun begins. My grandmother told me it was almost like a game of hide and seek or perhaps musical chairs, but if you keep watching every night and every morning you will soon discover that it will also tell you what the following days will bring.

I brought my wagon and team on down to the cabin and went in to grab some coffee and a couple of biscuits. Taking them back out onto the porch has always been my way to start the day, that is until old man winter comes knocking and that's when the table inside works just fine. As I sat on the porch finishing my last biscuit I noticed another line of clouds on past the ridge boiling up in the west like there might be something brewing for tonight. So I took my cup back inside, put out the fire then went back out to the wagon so I could get an early start on the firewood. My ride up the hill to the cutting area seemed to be so full of different signs for the changing season then last year. One sign that I found most folks wouldn't believe would be that of a wooly worm, the darker they are, the harshest the winter will be. This has been the story among most all Indian nations, but when the white man hears it, then its called just an old Indian tale. I guess they have never watched and listened like we do.

I could see all the downed trees just ahead spread out along the tree line next to the meadow. The air was also starting to get a little bit colder instead of warmer, but it shouldn't be that big of a deal because no sooner than I get to cutting the logs I'll sure be glad its cooler than hotter. I pulled up to where I thought was a good spot, grabbed my tools and went to work. A couple of hours have gone by already and it sure didn't seem to be warming up any, but then those clouds rolled in over the pass taking away my sunshine. I had a pretty good pile of wood laying there, at least two wagon loads from what I could tell. I walked back over to the wagon for some water then ventured on out into the meadow to get a better look at the sky. It was a solid gray with a colder wind starting to pick up, so with something moving in I had better start loading up the wagon and get back down to the cabin.

My horses were starting to get a little nervous over something and as I was walking over to them their nervousness turned into down right scared, they both acted as if they were going to break loose so I hurried over to them just in time for one closest to me to raise up and knock me for a loop. I jumped back up and managed to climb up onto the wagon so I could grab the reigns cause I knew they were going to break my tie down and I needed to be in control. Sure enough it broke loose from the tree and the wagon rodeo began. I held on and reigned with all I had till finally we came to a stop further out into the meadow.

I sat there looking all around for any reason why they were scared to the point of running away. Not seeing anything I held firm onto the reigns and with a slight snap steered them back over to where I was working. As I stood up on the wagon an ear piercing scream came shooting through the trees scaring the horses again, but this time they weren't staying at all. Their sudden departure sent me flying out of the wagon. There was no catching them this time as I sat there and watched my team and wagon heading back down the trail from where we came.

It didn't take me long to get over the runaway wagon when that scream of a mountain lion penetrated my ears again, except this time a little louder and a little closer. I stood as still as a scare crow looking into the woods then over at my rifle which was leaning against a tree about twenty feet away. I slowly started walking sideways towards the tree but still keeping my eyes moving back and forth hoping I can make it to my rifle before the cat shows himself. Then as I was within a few feet of the tree this large and more than likely hungry mountain lion came slowly creeping out of the trees with his eyes fixed directly on me. He kept walking towards me with his angry snarl so he could show me his main weapon of choice, long white fangs. By the way he was hunkered down I knew it would be any second now before he made his move on his next meal. Without moving my head I looked over to the rifle knowing I needed to make a long jump, grab the rifle, cock the lever, take aim and fire, all within a couple seconds. My heart was racing because when I make my move the cat will too.

I took what could be a final deep breath then jumped as hard as I could while reaching for the rifle before even hitting ground. Once having my rifle in hand I cocked the lever and rolled over to face the cat and take aim. There was no taking aim for the cat was already within his kill distance. I pulled the trigger just as he made his jump with the last thing I saw was his teeth and long sharp claws stretched out in front of him. It felt like a tree had fallen on top of me, a screaming tree with long sharp branches. The struggle lasted only a few moments then suddenly stopped. I laid on the ground with this heavy mountain lion on top of me and neither one of us moving a muscle. Not knowing what had happened, was I dead or was he, I then started to move my arms and the cat still didn't move. So with a loud yell I shoved the lion aside and rolled out from under him pointing my rifle at his head in case there was any movement at all from him.

The lion laid there just as still as could be, then I noticed some blood on the ground next to his chest. I grabbed his front leg rolling him over just enough to see that the one round I got off had struck him dead center of the chest. Thinking I was in the clear, a sharp pain in my shoulder and arm kept growing ever so stronger. Pulling my shirt back I saw the lion had made his mark on me before meeting his demise. My left shoulder had puncture wounds from his teeth and claw marks going down my arm. Now that the rush of survival was over my concentration went to my wounds making them even more painful. I needed to stop the bleeding but all I had to spare was my neck rag as a wrapping, but from the looks of my blood soaked shirt, I needed more than that. Looking around I saw a small grove of young aspen saplings. Knowing the ground around them would be moist I went over and started digging with a stick till I found some moist clay. Pulling my mostly ripped shirt off I started rubbing the dirt onto the wounds then packed some more on to help it seal. Once it started to dry I took what was left of the good side of the shirt and began wrapping tightly my shoulder and arm. I started walking back over where this fight had ended but it seems I had lost enough blood that my legs were becoming weak along with dizziness where I felt like I was stepping in a hole with every step. I was trying my best to not pass out but it just wasn't working because the last thing I saw was a dead mountain lion and then a cloudy sky.

I don't know how long I was out but I awoke almost freezing and hearing the wind blow through the trees like a train. It was almost dark with no stars or moon in the sky and I couldn't see any more than twenty yards ahead of me. My shirt was wrapped around my wounds and my jacket was in the wagon which hopefully was intact and back at the ranch by now. It isn't like this firewood was out back of the cabin, which would had been nice, no I had to come several miles up towards the pass to get the best dried wood. I never saw this coming when I was having coffee on the porch.

With what little light I had left there would be no possibility of walking back to the ranch tonight.

It would be pitch dark in a storm and then trying to keep the bleeding from starting up again. So I started stacking some logs against a couple of trees till I made a shelter then laid several of the branches over the top. At least I could crawl in there to keep out of the freezing wind. One last thing to do and that was to grab hold of the mountain lion and drag him over to the opening of the logs. The thought of what I needed to do before dragging him over wasn't that great, but I had to do it. I pulled my knife and began to clean out his carcass and take all the insides further away from my shelter. I do not need to be awakened by another hungry critter, instead I was hoping they will be drawn to the scent further out and down wind.

Trying to accomplish this by using one arm is not just awkward, but downright painful when I'm forced to use the wounded arm also. By now most all my light has gone so I hunkered down to a crawl and grabbed hold of the lion then started dragging him over to my pile of firewood. I brought him to the opening of the pile then I crawled inside pushing some leaves and sticks around till I could reach back out to once again take hold of my trophy, or in this case, my life saver through the night. I stretched my good arm out and pulled the lion closer to the opening with his belly side facing me so I could feel what little heat he had left in him. Once I couldn't feel the harsh wind any more I ended my struggle and laid back feeling as if all my strength had been completely drained.

It felt as if I had sunk into the ground with my arms and legs having no feeling to the touch, yet I could smell the mountain lion within inches beside me and feel what little warmth he had left hoping it would last through the night, but I knew it wouldn't. While listening to the wind outside of my cramped little shelter it seemed to ease my tension and quest for survival, it seemed soothing and my thoughts went to memories of the years past and gave me hope that I will awake in the morning.

I must have passed out right after closing the opening to my little shelter. Waking up came very slow and disoriented cause I could feel the sharp twigs under my back and hear the dried leaves crinkle as I tried to move and stretch my back. That was the part that told me I was not in my bed at the cabin and the reality of last night was taking hold. But for how long I wondered did I sleep because its still dark and I felt as if I had plenty of rest. The cold and stiff mountain lion was still up against the opening just like I had placed him. I started to push him away but he wouldn't budge at all and it was to small in here to bring my legs around to use my feet and push. I started prying between him and the logs till finally something was starting to give. I had pushed him away far enough only to seal it back up again with snow. This was not just a little flurry of snow, it was packed and had more than likely covered my entire shelter. But I kept on digging and pushing till I finally broke through what seemed to be an endless amount of snow only to see a blizzard of blowing snow with high winds that would knock you down. There was enough light to tell me it was the next day, but not a day for the walking wounded.

I quickly crawled back inside and pulled back the lion as far as I could then layed there waiting for one of the best ideas I have ever come up with, but looking around in this small area, which could also be my tomb, my mind was drawing a blank. My eyes were racing back and forth where I lay, and I was getting colder by the minute. Then my eyes stopped wandering as I stared at the hide of the mountain lion beside me. Without hesitation I managed to retrieve my knife and started cutting away the hide of the lion. Trying to turn him in all directions and pushing at the same time in order to break him loose from the frozen ground. This was the only chance I had to keep from being frozen and not found till spring. Then finally the hide came loose and I pulled it into the shelter covering my frozen body. This lion was getting ready to take my life, but now he may have saved it.

The hide was thick with a heavy coat of fur which would be a wonderful trophy to show off any other time. But its purpose now is to keep me warm and alive. I dozed in and out of sleep for what seemed forever hoping the next time I tried digging out of here the blizzard had let up so I can make an attempt to get back home. After a while it was a little bit lighter and not a sound, in fact it was complete silence. Hoping that was a good sign I started pushing the lion and snow away from the opening. I began digging upwards thinking the snow was pretty deep and I would get to the outside a lot sooner. It was beginning to get brighter in front of me as I dug even faster, then my hand broke through the snow pack and I finally saw daylight through the opening. I held onto the lion hide as I worked my way to the daylight while making the opening large enough for me to climb out. I crawled out of shelter rolling over into the deep snow looking at pure white all around. It was a big difference from when I rode up here and as far as I can figure that would have been yesterday morning.

The snow was still coming down but the blizzard winds had past leaving drifts that could swallow a man whole if you stepped in it. Able to move around now I took my knife and cut a slit in the center of the hide so I could stick my head through it and wrap the rest of the hide around me and tie it up. I looked over to the tunnel I had crawled out of and couldn't see any of the firewood shelter, the lion or any of the logs I had cut up, they were covered with at least two feet of snow. Then I remembered my Winchester, the best rifle I ever had is buried somewhere within only a few feet from where I am. Somewhere between these two trees and the my shelter is the last place I can remember having it in my hands. I laid on my good side pushing my arm as far as possible into to snow feeling around with my fingers. I did this in several spots then suddenly my effort paid off when I could feel the solid metal barrel of my rifle. When I retrieved my rifle from the deep snow I felt as if anything I did from here on out would get me closer to home.

With my rifle in hand and a new lion hide secured I started down the mountain. At this pace when every step you take sinks into the snow almost up to your knees, what normally would be a half a days walk could turn out to be two days. The snow is still falling steadily but not as heavy as earlier when I came out of that snowy grave. I would turn and look back ever so often to see how far I had traveled, but that same grove of aspen were still within my site. Good gosh almighty, its as if I were walking backwards. About every twenty steps I would stand still in my tracks out of exhaustion and tempted to lean back onto the snow for a small amount of rest. But I still had enough sense left in me I knew that would be a frozen and fatal choice. I had to keep walking no matter how deep the snow or how cold it became.

After a while the snow was getting lighter and so was the sky. I was able to see further ahead to where I recognized all the tree lines and the mountain sides. I was born and raised in these mountains and I have rode every square mile of them from the Greenhorn to the Monarchs, but I cant remember once when I walked through it in two feet of snow wearing a mountain lion pelt while having a shredded arm and shoulder. This sure as shoot wasn't by choice but as I thought of everything that had happened to me over the past several hours or perhaps days, and came up with one thing for sure. What could have been a disaster for my horses and certain death for me, the Great Spirit provided me shelter and warmth. And now I have no doubt that same faith will take me back to my porch.

Step after step was starting to be so routine I hadn't even noticed that the snow had stopped and it was getting brighter. I stopped for a while looking all around and could see a few openings in clouds with blue skies behind them. A smile came over my face as I stood there looking upwards at the clouds slowly moving away and more clearings on the way. The warmth of the sun would sure feel awfully good right now.

I was hoping it wouldn't happen , but I believe

with the pain in my feet along with numbness, a bit of frostbite is starting to set in. No matter how much the sun will shine, my feet will still be buried in this snow. I have been through this same thing several winters ago but it hasn't stopped me yet. I can still walk, run, ride and for sure step into two feet of snow all day long. Then as the clouds were trying to tell me earlier, they started moving aside so the sun can make his appearance. The sun was off to my left and high in the sky which told me it was still morning and I had a full day ahead. In all this snow I knew my speed wouldn't pick up but my spirits certainly did.

I tried to keep looking downward, not just so I would see where I was stepping but the glare from the sun on all this snow. As much as the sun seemed to be a blessing for my quest to make it back, it can now also be a burden to your sight. I remember one time up in the Dakotas my cousin Standing Bear told me that not only was the facial paint a symbol of strength, but under your eyes it would help give you sight by stopping the glare of the sun. As I kept moving forward in this blinding snow I had no idea where to find anything except to dig down into the soil and bring up some dirt to smear on my face. So I started moving around till I cleared out a space in the snow big enough that I could dig down and find some dirt. I did just that but what I found was a frozen ground, even with my knife I retrieved only a small amount but not enough to wipe on without it falling right off. Then with the knife still in my hand another thought came to me. I made a small cut on my finger and squeezed till blood appeared then wiped it under each of my eyes. This seemed to work a little because some of the glare was starting to go away and the cold was also stopping the bleeding from the cut. It was working so well that I kept on going able to see a little better and hoping it stays on long enough without needing to cut myself ever so often.

I have made it around the first bend beyond the trees heading out into another meadow. Because of constantly stepping high my legs were starting to loose a lot of strength which has caused me to fall to my knees several times, also loosing what dried blood I had on my face to help kill the glare. About half way into this meadow is a fairly deep ravine, but just wide enough that you can still jump it on horse back, which I have done several times. It will make a few turns and then start to flatten out a little further down where I always cross especially with the wagon. I am trying everything to cover my eyes yet still be able to see ahead where the trees and large boulders lay. I can pretty much judge the distance between these places as to where the ravine would be, but even still I will lower each step into the snow very carefully, if nothing is there then back the heck up.

The thoughts that go through your mind while trying to stay alive would keep anyone out of trouble if you can only think of them while everything is good. But why would you think to bring extra clothing, matches, or even some shaded eye glasses just to go cut some firewood on a normal yet cloudy day. I have all of those things back at the cabin, so shame on me for not putting them in the wagon with me, cause they certainly would have made this stroll through the mountains a lot more tolerable.

Right now I have got to stop for just a few moments to rest my legs and my eyes. So once again I started moving around and packing snow down around me till I was able to sit down and cup my face into my hands. My eyes felt as if they were burning and full of dust so I knew that the snow blindness was starting to take a toll on me. If I can just keep them closed and rested for a little while, then perhaps I can make out the landmarks a lot better than I can now. The sun was shining on the back of my neck making me feel a lot warmer but also making me want to lay back and close my eyes even longer. I had to get back up and continue walking no matter how painful or tired because the alternative could be worse.

Finding my rifle in the snow turned out to be a

blessing in several ways and not just a weapon, because today I have used it for a prop and a balancing weight. I held the barrel and pushed to raise myself up from my little resting spot and immediately began squinting my eyes till they were almost shut. I didn't believe when I set out on this adventure that I would start preying for clouds, but unless there is some relief I will have full snow blindness in less than an hour. I would look upward into the sky hoping to see a cloud or two, but it was clear in all directions. Even looking up helped my sight because there was no snow glare, but trying to look up the entire time your walking is like walking through a cactus patch blindfolded.

The blindness has worsened and I had no choice but to stop dead in my tracks and try everything I could to help me carry on. I tried a little snow against my eyes to help ease the burning feeling, but all that seemed to do was make my eyes cold, but then, why wouldn't it. I found myself laughing out loud at some of my ideas and then talking out loud by asking if I thought something would work and then answering myself by whether it would or not. Even though I wasn't realizing it, the fatigue and the snow blindness was joining forces to turn this old cowboy into a basket case. There is a lot of similar conditions from crossing a desert with nothing but sand and sunshine before you for miles and walking across a blinding snow for miles. At least in the snow I am not thirsty and in the desert I am not frozen. But the way everything else works on your spirit is very much the same.

I stood there trying my best to see anything and at the same time digging deep into my thoughts to take control of my thinking. I wasn't able to see anything at all, no distinctive shapes or distance of any kind. I only knew that it was still daylight. But then suddenly a darker figure appeared in front of me, a large figure that was moving about from side to side. My first thought was, surly not a bear cause in my condition, the odds are against me.

I held my rifle waving it back and forth in front of me and shouting out any rebel yell I could, knowing that if it were a bear, what ever you said didn't mean a darn thing to them, so all I could do was prepare myself for another fight to the death and hope the victor was myself. As I stood there in readiness with my rifle waiting for the first blow I heard a sound that was sweet music to my heart. It was that of a horse whinnying and snorting while moving about. This wasn't any horse either, it was Ruger, I would know him anywhere and at anytime. This had surprised me so much that all I could do was call out his name, "RUGER, RUGER!! Is that you boy". I cant remember a time when I had been so happy and excited over something I couldn't even see. With my arms stretched outward and calling his name I soon felt his snout against my chest nudging and snorting. With my arms already stretched outward I was able to close them in around his neck hugging him tightly and feeling his warmth while he shook his head up and down. After several moments of this wonderful greetings and still holding tight around his neck the thoughts of how could this be, and how did he know where to go was my thoughts. But at this time why should I question any of those thoughts because I have always said that a mans best friend is his horse and in this case and many others this is as true as heaven above. I threw my arm over Rugers neck and pulled myself up and onto his back. I sat there not being able to see anything around except a shadow here and there with what little vision I had. But none of that mattered anymore because I felt as safe as anyone could and warmer than I have ever felt. With my left hand I grabbed a hand full of Rugers mane and sat up on his back as tall and straight as I could. The pain of frostbite and mountain lion wounds seemed to have disappeared along with any thoughts of my friend Buck searching the area only to find me frozen under the snow. I gave Ruger a gentle nudge and told him, "Lets go home boy". He swung his head around to touch my leg, then we walked slowly down the mountain towards home.

CHAPTER 6

Thoughts From The Saddle

SOMETIMES A MAN will search beyond his heart and soul to find something greater in life than what he has at the time. I believe these thoughts are something anyone would put aside after they witness a new foal opening its eyes then try to stand on those small and frail legs. Maybe even after calving season when you look upon several new faces peering out from among the tall new grass. As I look over my north pasture witnessing all the new life coming to my ranch I can only hope and pray that one day someone will see the same dream that I have started then carry it on for the next new cowboy to live his dream and accomplish his goals.

So as I sit here relaxed in my saddle looking out over my home while the evening sun is slowly sinking into the mountain pass behind me and watching the shadow of myself and my horse slowly becoming larger across the land before me. Call me crazy, but I feel it is a sign that God is marking my home with something as simple as my shadow. So with that as my thoughts and gut feeling, how can I dispute it with anything else, I won't. But I will as sure as the world be up here again tomorrow morning feeling the same and ready to take on another day.

CPSIA information can be obtained
at www.ICGtesting.com
Printed in the USA
FSOW01n2115070118
43159FS